The Weeping Bridge

GHOST HUNTERS SOCIETY

Book One

Adria Waters

For Mom and Dad who lovingly support all my adventures

CHAPTER 1

Don't barf, don't barf, don't barf. I peered out the passenger window, the red and yellow trees a blur as we drove along the hilliest, curviest road ever made. I tried to focus on a cloud, still and quiet in the sky. Staring at it, I hoped that I could calm my stomach through willpower alone. Dad had offered me some antacid from the glove compartment an hour ago, but the medicine was almost two months past its expiration date and I had decided to take my chances with the hills and curves.

Big mistake.

The car hit a rise, jolting me up and down, my stomach ending up somewhere in my throat.

Dad glanced over at me. "Sorry," he mumbled. "We're almost there."

I burped. The taste of sour bacon from the BLT I ate somewhere around Columbia filled my mouth. "Not...gonna...make it!" I was already fumbling with the handle of the door by the time Dad wrestled the car to the shoulder. I made it to the guardrail before my lunch escaped. Tears streamed from my eyes as the contents of my stomach ended up in the weeds along the side of the road. I heaved once more, gulping down huge breaths of the crisp afternoon air as I let my forehead rest against the cool metal.

The car door slammed behind me and gravel crunched as Dad came around the car. "Breathe in through your nose and out through your mouth. Just relax." He smoothed my hair back from my face in an awkward motion. "Don't worry. Not a soul out here to see you toss your cookies."

No kidding. We hadn't seen another vehicle on the narrow two-lane road for the last twenty minutes. I took another deep breath and allowed the fresh air and stillness to calm my roiling stomach as I climbed up to sit on the guardrail. I clasped my clammy hands together tightly, and for about the millionth time since leaving St. Louis, wished that my mom was here. She would have smiled and told me it was all going to be okay. Well, she would have, if she hadn't gone and died on us five months ago.

Dad draped his heavy wool blazer around my shoulders and sat down next to me on the guardrail. He took out a butterscotch candy and examined it thoughtfully for a moment before unwrapping it, the crinkling the only sound for miles. He shoved the wrapper in his pocket and stared out over the hills. Most dads would have taken this opportunity to tout the character-building aspects of this new adventure we were on, or tell me that I would make new friends and settle right in, or convince me that leaving my whole world behind to start a new life at Grandma and Grandpa's old farm was going to be wonderful. Not my dad, though. He sat quietly, rolling the candy in his mouth and scanning the scene around him. For that, I was eternally grateful.

Tears sprang to my eyes and I wiped at them roughly with the back of my hand. I glanced at Dad to see if he had noticed. I hated crying in front of him. The setting sun shone through the trees, casting an orange glow on his graying hair. In the months since Mom got sick, his hair had gone from shiny brown to salt and pepper gray and the lines on his face had deepened. The biggest change, though, was in his eyes. Even when he smiled, his eyes had a wistful sadness in them. I wondered if my eyes looked the same.

Dad stood up. "Ready?"

I shrugged off his blazer and handed it back to him. "I guess so." The truth was, I wasn't ready for any of this. I wasn't ready for my mom to die. I wasn't ready to say goodbye to our house, my school, or my best friend. I wasn't ready to move halfway across the state and I certainly wasn't ready to transfer during my junior year to a new high school.

No one asked me, though.

Dad reached out a hand to help me from my perch. "We really are getting close now." He walked around the car and opened his door. Cocking his head to the side, he regarded me over the roof. "You excited?"

"I'm not sure excited is the word I would use." I got in, pushing the pile of magazines on the floorboard to the side, making room for my feet. "I'm..." I considered while Dad fired up the engine and nosed the car back onto the highway, "...guardedly optimistic."

Dad raised an eyebrow my way and snorted.

My phone hadn't gotten a decent signal since leaving the interstate, so I opened the latest edition of my favorite science magazine to an article about the development of three-dimensional art. It allowed people who were without sight to experience the great works of artists. I pulled my legs up into the car seat and hunkered down over the pages.

When it got too dark to read a little while later, I gave up and shoved the magazine into my backpack. I looked out into the gathering darkness. The landscape of northwest Missouri was filled with wide open spaces that alternated with small forests of scraggly trees. It was hillier here than home and felt wilder somehow. I missed the lights and sounds of the city.

"How come we never visited Grandma and Grandpa while they were alive?" I asked. I had vague memories of them visiting us in St. Louis, sitting uncomfortably on our leather couch, steaming mugs of coffee in their hands.

Dad glanced over. "They visited us a couple of times when you were little."

I shrugged. "I remember."

"Your grandparents were never happy when they were off the farm. They worried about the crops and the animals." He glanced over again.

"How come we didn't visit them?"

"We were busy."

"And, you didn't want to come here."

It was several minutes before he answered. I thought maybe I'd stepped over some unspoken boundary.

"No, I didn't. I had wonderful memories of this place and I didn't want to taint those memories." He pressed his lips into a thin line. "Dad hated that I left the farm. He always wanted me to take it over. It took us a long time to come to terms, and by that time, your mom and I were working crazy hours to get our careers started. Before we knew it, we ran out of time."

Grandma and Grandpa died within two weeks of each other. Mom used to say that one could never stand to be without the other. I looked down at my hands.

Dad was quiet for a long time. "Your grandma and grandpa loved you."

The conversation was over. We sat in silence another fifteen minutes before turning onto a lonely two lane highway.

"I know the driveway's along here somewhere. Been a while since I've come in this way. We should have left earlier," Dad said, almost to himself. He leaned over the dashboard, his glasses nearly tapping on the windshield as he scanned the side of the road for a break in the underbrush. I tried to help, squinting into the fading evening light, not sure exactly what I was looking for.

"There it is!" Dad pointed to a gravel road leading off into a line of trees that hid everything beyond from view. He eased the wheels from the blacktop onto the gravel and we jostled along slowly, listening to the car's shocks squeak and groan in protest. As we rounded the corner, Dad slowed the car to a crawl.

"Um, Dad...shouldn't we keep going?" I looked around. "It's getting dark and the majority of car accidents happen between the hours of three and six p.m."

Dad mumbled something about having seen the last of rush hours for a long time. Then, he nodded to the front of the car. "See it?" he asked.

I followed his gaze and got my first look at the place where my dad had grown up.

A whitewashed two-story farmhouse sat in a valley, flanked by two massive hills covered in trees. The driveway snaked its way up to the house, the white gravel glowing iridescent in the moonlight. A gigantic tree anchored the front yard and spread its branches protectively over the roof while rosebushes hugged the front porch in a gentle embrace.

I exhaled the breath I didn't realize I had been holding. *This wasn't so bad, right?* After all of Dad's descriptions of his boyhood home, I hadn't been sure what to expect. So far, it was totally picturesque from a distance. I had a sneaking suspicion, though, that this was going to be the best it would look to us for a while.

I was right.

As we got closer, Dad must have felt the need to provide a running dialogue that only helped to make my outlook bleaker by the minute. "Well, that fence will need to be repaired, and the garden will need to be tilled under before the winter. See those shingles on the roof? I hope it hasn't leaked yet. We'll have to get to that first. Look there. The doors need fixing on that old barn."

We rolled up to the house and Dad cut the engine. He got out and walked to the front of the car, leaning against the hood. I grabbed my jacket from the backseat and wrapped it tightly around me before venturing out of the car. The night was crisp. Autumn was in full swing already in mid-October and Dad said he thought it would be a cold winter. I walked around to the front of the car and leaned against the warm hood next to him.

"We're here," Dad said, his voice soft. "You know, Peanut, when your grandma and grandpa left it to me, I always thought I would sell it. I never really thought we'd be living here..." He trailed off.

"Well," I tried to smile, but my mouth didn't seem to be working correctly, "if it makes you feel any better, Dad, neither did I."

He put his arm around my shoulders and squeezed. "Shall we go in?" He started up the wooden steps of the wide front porch, continuing to tick off a checklist that was sure to keep me void of free time until next year.

I could see a few lights dotting the night, but no close houses and certainly no neighbors milling around walking their dogs or putting out the trash. Our old neighborhood in Créve Coeur had been full of people. My best friend, Piper, only lived three houses down from our brick two-story. When we were little, we used to spend almost every night at one or the other's house. Then, after Mom got sick, Piper quit coming around as much. She said it made her too sad to see my mother propped up in the hospital bed in the living room.

I took a deep breath and shook my head, clearing it. "How close are we to the nearest town?" I looked up at the sky and turned in a circle. The stars hung in a curtain above me. I could never see this many stars at night in St. Louis and I added this as the first entry of my pros column. I usually always had some sort of a pros and cons worksheet going on in my mind – about everything. So far, moving to Culvers Grove, Missouri had a very unbalanced list.

"Well, Eagleton is pretty close and the nearest bigger town is Chillicothe." Dad pointed vaguely to the southeast.

"How far are we from Kansas City then?"

"Oh, I'd say about a couple hours or so."

My stomach sank and I stopped spinning. There was going to be nothing to do here. No art museums, no concerts, no friends. I trudged up the steps behind him.

Dad jiggled his key up and down and finally got the door unlocked. It opened with a rusty squeal. Whispers escaped from the vacant house and wound around my head, then rose into the sky above me. I batted a hand at them, shooing them away. They didn't belong here, but then again, neither did I.

Dad reached inside and flipped the light switch near the door up and down. "Hmmm, doesn't look like the electricity is on. Better get the flashlights." He trotted down the steps to the car, not even noticing that I was still standing on the porch, my mouth hanging open. *Did he really just say there wasn't even electricity?* I mean, moving to the boonies was one thing, but I had no intention of staying way out here with no lights. No way. That was exactly how the *one* horror movie Piper had talked me into watching started.

The porch swing moved in the breeze and goosebumps broke out along my arms. "You know, if you wanted to hurry with those flashlights, that would be totally cool," I said under my breath. I wrapped my arms around me and looked over my shoulder. Something was watching me from the overgrown garden. It was a feeling I was familiar with. You'd think I'd be used to it by now. Scared that I would see something looking back if I stared too long, I turned around and plastered my back against the front of the house. The peeling paint snagged at my jacket. I took a deep breath and focused on driving away the feeling.

Dad strode up the steps, shining two flashlight beams in front of him. One of the beams swept past his face and I thought he looked almost happy, something I hadn't seen since Mom had gotten sick. I took another deep breath and vowed to try to like it here as I followed him into the house.

After all, things couldn't get much worse, right?

Turns out, I was wrong about that, too. Not only was there no electricity, but there was also no heat. An animal had built a nest in the flue and when Dad tried to light a fire, the smoke billowed into the liv-

ing room, driving us both outside onto the porch until it cleared. With no real furniture in the house and
the moving truck not due until the next afternoon,
I calmly and rationally suggested that we stay at a
hotel for the evening.

Dad looked at me. "I'd rather take my chances
with the animals here. You want to look around a
little bit?"

"Are you coming with me?"

He smiled and put his arm around my shoulders
again. "Of course, you big chicken."

Behind the living room was a dining room that
led to a spacious kitchen. Off the kitchen was a mudroom that had two doors: one to the screened in back
porch and one that led to the basement. I balked at
the stairs.

"We can look down there tomorrow morning."
Dad closed the door and shone his flashlight at the
stairs that led to the second floor. "You want me to
go first?"

I nodded and followed him, my steps light on the
worn wooden treads. Upstairs, two bedrooms
flanked a large bathroom and a huge room spanned
the front of the house. All the furniture had been
sold at auction, except a couple of chairs and a massive dresser in the smaller bedroom. We went down

the other set of stairs. These led back into the hall-way, dumping us out between a bathroom on the left of the landing and a room with glass French doors on the right. A master bedroom and another bath-room were at the rear of the house, the lace curtains hanging limply from the crooked rod in the room.

"Electricity, then heat, then furniture. It'll feel more like a real house by the end of the weekend." Dad looked at me, rubbing his chin. "We're going to be all right."

I pulled out my phone and tried to send a text to Piper to let her know we'd gotten here, but it wouldn't go through. "I know," I mumbled. I sighed and shoved my phone back in my pocket.

"Wi-Fi's right after furniture, okay?" Dad un-rolled the sleeping bag he had brought in from the trunk and fixed up a pallet for me on the living room floor.

I kicked off my tennis shoes and sat down on the sleeping bag. "Where are you going to sleep?" I would never admit it, but I hoped he would say something like, "Less than twelve feet away from you so you won't be scared."

"I'm going to see if I can get the water running in the bathroom so we can at least wash our faces in the morning and then I'll probably bunk down over there." He gestured absently to a misshapen recliner in the corner of the room. Grabbing both flashlights, he handed me one and then walked down the hallway. I watched the beam of his flashlight play on the faded wallpaper and then dim as he went into the bathroom. After a whole day of travel in the car, I was exhausted. I pulled my hair out of the ponytail holder and rolled my head on my shoulders. My neck popped. Flipping off the flashlight, I snuggled down into the sleeping bag and turned over on my side.

At first, I wasn't sure what I was seeing. The person at the front window turned and disappeared like a shadow into the darkness beyond. I let out a strangled scream and fumbled to turn on my flashlight. In my terror, I ended up dropping it and knocking it across the floor.

"Dad! Dad! There's someone out there! Hurry!" I yanked at the zipper on my sleeping bag to no avail.

A second later, Dad skidded into the living room, aiming his flashlight right at me. "Where?"

"Right there! There was a face looking in at me!"

Dad strode past me, yanked open the door, and stepped out onto the porch. He shone his flashlight beam back and forth across the empty yard. I finally managed to free myself from the tangle of the sleeping bag and rolled out unceremoniously, grabbing my tennis shoes and clambering out onto the porch.

"Wait here," Dad said. "I'm going to look around."

"No way!" I grabbed his arm. "I'm coming with you."

We walked down the creaking wooden steps of the porch and out into the yard. The wind had picked up and whipped my hair around my eyes. I stopped to pull it into a loose knot and then caught up with my dad. We walked all over the yard, checking out the barn, the corncrib, and a half dozen other buildings that I had no idea what they were used for. Finally, he turned to me and asked the inevitable, "Are you *sure* you saw someone?"

For a moment, I wasn't. Things like that happened to me all the time. I felt guilty for scaring him and then angry because he didn't believe me. A million answers to his question floated around in my head: *No, I thought it would be fun to wander around outside in the middle of the night* or *I thought I'd add some excitement to your life* or *the solitude of this place is already driving me crazy.* One look at my dad's earnest face, though, and I swallowed my sarcastic comments.

"Whatever," I murmured, turning and heading back into the house. "Maybe I was wrong. It could have been the wind."

As we walked back inside, I looked out the door once more. No, I was sure I had seen someone. Someone with green eyes and a tangle of long black hair. I wasn't sure who she was, but I was definitely going to find out.

CHAPTER 2

The next morning dawned very cold. I woke up shivering. Dad's blanket was already folded neatly on the arm of the empty chair, half a dozen candy wrappers lying on top. I smiled as I picked them up and shoved them in my pocket. He quit smoking the day Mom had gotten the diagnosis but was too stubborn to use the patch.

I gathered the sleeping bag around me and wandered through the house, looking for him. Now that it was light, I could see the interior and while it showed some signs of wear, it really wasn't that bad considering my grandparents had passed away three years before, leaving it vacant. I could already picture my dad's office in the room with the glass doors and imagined his heavy desk in the space. I shuffled through the dining room and into the sunny kitchen, the zipper of the sleeping bag dragging across the faded green linoleum.

"Dad?" I called up the stairs in the kitchen.

"Out here!" came the response from the back yard.

I looked out the window above the sink and saw that Dad had already pulled the car into its parking spot behind the house. He was busy cleaning it out.

I stepped onto the bright sun porch. "Gee, are we leaving already?" I asked through the screen door.

"Nice try!" He paused, resting the bottom of a box against the back bumper. "We need to go into town to take care of some things. First off, I'm going to need some help out here, so we'll need to hire someone."

"Are you taking requests? I'd like tall, dark, and handsome, please."

Dad laughed. The way it echoed in the valley made it seem like he was laughing all around me. It was comforting and safe. "Go get dressed, okay? We're leaving in ten minutes so we can be back out here to meet the movers this afternoon."

"Fine, but I don't have to go all mountain man like you, do I?" I eyed his jeans and flannel shirt.

"You couldn't pull off this look as well as me!" He smiled and struck a pose. "Now go get ready."

Ten minutes later, I was still shivering from my cold splash in the sink as we drove along the gravel driveway to the two-lane road we arrived on last night. This time, we turned right and followed the road as it rose gently over the hills. The sun hovered above the horizon, spreading its warm red glow over glistening leaves tinged in frost.

"Think it might get warm today?" I asked.

Dad considered for a moment. "Maybe. The weatherman was calling for a warm up this week."

As we drove, I pulled down the sunshield and put on mascara and lip-gloss while Dad went over his list of things that needed to be done to make the house livable for us. For a while, we traveled along a four lane highway and then turned west again before driving over a hill into a tiny town. Dad stopped at the intersection and turned left at the stop sign.

"Culvers Grove," my dad read the sign as we rolled past. "Home of the State Champion Bobcats."

I groaned inwardly as I looked out on the deathly quiet town square. *More like "The Town that Time Forgot."*

We drove along the deserted Main Street, passing a brown stone building on the corner with a sign above the door that read, "Post Office." Next to that was a restaurant with a bright blue awning with Calico Café painted in large block letters. A massive courthouse stood in the middle of the square, its red brick worn but well maintained. The streets were dotted with a few cars and trucks parked facing the sidewalks, and the parking meters were clad in dried corn stalks. The small storefronts we passed boasted decorated windows full of pumpkins and fall leaves.

Farther down Main Street, my dad nudged his Mercedes into a diagonal parking space along the sidewalk in front of a hardware store. We got out and slammed the doors, looking around. *All this needs are a few tumbleweeds.* No one was out on the street yet. Maybe it was too early. The sign over the bank told me that it was 7:43 a.m. and the temperature was forty-two degrees. There were no lights on in the hardware store and my dad leaned close to check out the hours.

"Well, kiddo," he stood up and squinted down the street, "it doesn't open for about twenty minutes. You wanna grab a bite at the diner?" He gestured toward the restaurant with a hand inside his jacket pocket and then led the way down the sidewalk. On the window of the diner, someone had painted "GO BOBCATS!" in shoe polish. Underneath was a painting of what resembled an alley cat that had been run over by a truck ten or twenty times. I snorted and Dad opened the door for me. A small bell jangled and a waitress with blue jeans and a blond ponytail bounced out from behind the counter, a huge smile on her face.

"Well, hey there!" She chomped on a piece of neon yellow gum and looked from my dad to me. "Can you believe this weather we're having? That's Missouri for you, warm one day and freezing the next! My granddaddy used to say, 'Don't like the weather? Give it a minute – it'll change!' Haven't seen you all in town. Are you guys visiting? Do you have relatives here?" As she kept up her chatter, she gathered two menus and silverware rolls and led us to a booth near the big front window. She put the menus and rolls on the table and stood there with her hands on her hips. "My name's Jessica. What do you guys wanna drink? Coffee? Soda? Lemonade? Juice? I think we got some orange juice or apple juice."

"Um, I'll have lemonade," I mumbled, pulling off my jacket and trying to wrangle my unwashed hair into a ponytail holder.

"And I'll have coffee. Two creams." Dad held up two fingers.

Jessica pulled out a pen and scratched on a note-pad. She stopped mid-stroke and cocked her head to the side. "So, are you guys the family moving into the old Anderson place? You know, we've all been wondering what was gonna happen to that place now that old Mister and Missus Anderson are gone. Seems like they lived in this town forever. My mama said their family was one of the first families here in Culvers Grove." She smiled, tapping the end of her pen on her tablet absently. The noise echoed in the almost empty diner.

"I'm John and this is Marissa, and yes, we are moving into the old Anderson place. It's where I grew up." Dad smiled. "Do you go to the high school here?"

"Cool! Yeah, I'm a junior." She turned to me and regarded me with perfectly made up blue eyes. "How about you?"

"Junior, too," I said.

"Oh, if you're not busy later, I can take you over to sign up for school. I'm off here at nine anyway so I can go with Mom to Chillicothe to shop for Daddy's birthday present. I'll check, but I'm sure Shawn will let me off here early and Mom won't mind if I'm late, especially when I tell her I met you two. Everybody in town's been speculating about you guys ever since we heard you were moving back to Culvers Grove."

"I'm not sure..." I started.

Dad nodded in my direction. "Go ahead. I have plenty to do in town until you get back."

"O-okay," I said. "It's Saturday. Will the school be open?"

"Absolutely! It's open nearly every weekend starting, gosh, even before football season so the guys can practice. Football's a pretty big deal around here. We were ten and oh last year and we've won our first game already this year. I'm a cheer-leader." She blushed. "I'm sorry. I haven't even taken your order yet and you guys must be starving. My boyfriend, Rick, says I talk too much, but isn't it just like a boy to think everyone talks too much even if they don't? So have you guys decided?"

We both ordered eggs and pancakes. When Jessica walked away to put in our order, Dad leaned over. "You okay with this? I think it might be good for you to meet some people around here. Won't make Monday seem so bad and all."

"It's no problem." I picked at a ball of fuzz on my sweater sleeve. The truth was thinking about meeting people here meant that we would actually be staying in Culvers Grove and I didn't think I was ready to accept that yet. It meant leaving everything else from my previous life behind: my house, my friends, and my mom. The last one hurt too much and I tried to think of something else while I looked out the window and blinked back tears.

I knew when Mom got sick almost a whole year ago now that things were going to change. When I came home from school that late December day and saw my parents' cars in the driveway, my stomach had immediately knotted. They were never home in the middle of the afternoon, especially not during the holiday months when they both put in long hours at their jobs. I ran up the front steps and through the door, dropping my backpack on the floor and shrugging off my coat.

"Mom! Dad!"

"We're in here, Marissa," came the reply from the kitchen. They were sitting at the table, holding steaming cups of coffee in oversized mugs, their faces somber and lined with worry.

"Come sit down, Peanut." Dad reached across the table to take my mom's hand.

My stomach dropped and I stood rooted to the spot. Something was really wrong. Were they going to get a divorce? They were always so happy, but then again, Piper said her parents had seemed happy right up until the morning her dad left. She never saw it coming.

"Come on, honey. Come sit down," Mom said. My stomach flip flopped as I pulled out a chair and sat, looking at my mom's nose, her impossibly straight nose, and wondering if I would ever be as pretty as she was.

"Marissa, your dad and I have something to tell you." My mom took a deep breath and let out a hitching sigh as she looked over at my dad. He leaned back in his chair, looking up at the ceiling, his impeccably ironed shirt wrinkling with the motion. Here it comes, I thought desperately. Divorce. I mean, why not? Lots of kids in my sophomore class at Parkview North had parents that were divorced. My parents had made a good run at it, right? They could part amicably, and as long as they lived near each other, I could continue to go to school and not much would change. I would have to keep half of my stuff at Mom's place and half at my dad's. Who would get the house? And, what would I do if I forgot my homework at one parent's or needed a certain outfit for school from the other's?

"It's okay, guys," I blurted out. "Forty-one percent of marriages end in divorce. Can I keep my books here or will I have to move them to Dad's place?"

A sad smile crept across my mom's face. "Oh, honey, no. Your dad and I aren't getting a divorce."

She looked over at my dad and squeezed his hand. His face looked ashen and he continued to look up at the ceiling. "Honey," she said, "do you remember a little while back, when I started feeling really tired all of the time?"

I nodded.

"Well, I went to the doctor yesterday and they ran some tests to find out why I'm not feeling well. Your dad and I got the results of those tests today. Now, I don't want you to worry, I know how you do." Mom reached over to touch my hand. "Marissa, honey, the doctors found cancer. They say that we can treat it aggressively with chemotherapy and radiation and..."

I didn't hear anything else. The whole world began moving in slow motion like in those cheesy movies where the main character gets some huge news and the audience is forced to pause while the character processes it all. But, I swear, that is exactly what happened. I could see my mother's mouth moving, shaping the words "pancreatic cancer" and "stage three" but the words were coming out muffled and she seemed so far away. I peered over at my dad and he was looking straight at me. His face was gray and his blue eyes watery. He tried to smile, but a tear spilled out instead and wound its way around the stubble on his cheek, finally dropping in a ring on his tie. He shoved his chair back and grabbed his blazer from the hook by the door. I watched as he stood out on the back porch and lit a cigarette, turning the filter around and around between his fingers the way he did when he was thinking hard about something. He tossed it into the backyard and stood outside, his hands shoved deep into the pockets of his blazer.

I turned back to my mom and she was still talking, but it sounded like she was speaking through cotton. All I could hear was the clock above the fridge clicking away the seconds in a steady staccato beat. *Tick, tick, tick.* I sat there listening to the clock as my mom told me about her treatment – the treatment that ultimately didn't work. The doctors tried to save her and she fought hard, right up until the end. Sixteen weeks after diagnosing my mother with cancer, they sent her home, telling us there was nothing to do but help keep her comfortable for the next few weeks. Then, one early morning, the end came.

I pushed the memory back down to its safe place inside me. If I didn't think about it, it was almost like it hadn't happened. Mom was away for a while. She would be back sometime and she would give me a hug and tell me she was sorry for leaving me alone. I glanced up at my dad.

He was bending two straw wrappers together. The creases between his eyes deepened with concentration. He caught me staring and smiled. "You okay?"

I nodded. "Yeah, I'm okay."

Jessica brought the food and sat down with us while we ate, chattering about the town and her boyfriend, and asking no less than a million questions about living in St. Louis. Finally, Dad finished his coffee and stood. While Jessica took the plates away, he shrugged on his jacket. "I'll be at the hardware store." He squinted out the window. "Looks like it's open now. How long do you think you'll be?"

Jessica appeared at our table with a bright purple purse thrown over her shoulder and keys jangling in her hand. "It should only take us about an hour. I figure I'll show her around the school if we have time after we pick up her books." She turned to me. "You ready?"

I nodded.

"Meet me at the hardware store when you get back into town. Do you have your phone?"

I nodded.

He looked over his glasses at me. "Is it charged?"

"Seventy-six percent."

Dad held the door open for Jessica and me before he headed down the sidewalk. I watched him for a moment, noticing for the first time how skinny he looked. His jacket practically engulfed him and his jeans were hanging in loose wrinkles around his legs. Losing Mom hadn't been easy on him. It hadn't been easy on either of us.

"Bye, Mr. Anderson!" Jessica grabbed my arm and pulled me down the sidewalk in the opposite direction. "Where did you get those jeans? They are so cool! None of the stores around here have anything to buy, like, ever!" Jessica stopped in front of a Jeep, a red monster covered in dried, caked on mud. "We took her out mudding the other night and it's been too cold to wash her, but today's supposed to be really nice, so we should run by the car wash." Jessica threw her apron in the back as she swung into the driver's seat. I climbed in the passenger side and searched for the seatbelt. Pulling out my phone to look up the safety rating on this car, I almost dropped it when Jessica turned the key and country music screamed out of her speakers into the quiet town square. She punched the gas, squealing her tires as she backed out onto the street. "I just got my license two weeks ago!" she yelled above the roar of the motor and the sound of the wind whipping through the open window. "Mom says she and Daddy couldn't be happier now that they don't have to drive me everywhere!"

Dad had finally convinced me to get mine last month. I told him that sixteen-year-olds had crash rates higher than any other age, but he had only smiled and told me that he didn't know any other driver, no matter what age, that would be as careful as I would be. We sped past the center of town and out onto a curvy two lane road. I grabbed onto the door handle and held on for dear life as Jessica floored it around a corner.

"So, why are you guys moving here, anyway?" The car swerved a bit as she leaned over to turn down the radio. "I tell you, if I lived in a city like St. Louis, I'd never move away!" The wind was whipping strands of Jessica's white blond hair out of her ponytail and around her face as she drove.

"After my mom got sick," I said, "Dad decided to sell our house and move here to where he grew up." I shrugged my shoulders, hoping that this would be explanation enough, but already knowing it wouldn't be.

"So, where's your mom now? You said she was sick? Like sick, pneumonia, or sick, schizophrenic?"

"She had cancer. She passed away in May."

Jessica snuck a sideways look at me. "I'm sorry. That really sucks."

What followed was approximately three and a half minutes of blissful silence as the Jeep sped down the road.

"Is that the school?" I pointed out the windshield.

Jessica brightened, seemingly glad to have something to break the awkward silence. I was used to it. No one ever knew what to say. Heck, neither did I most of the time. "Yeah, the elementary school is there," she pointed, "and the high school is there."

The squat red brick buildings were connected by a breezeway. The parking lot was massive and flanked the high school on two sides. It looked decent enough. Small, but not the one room schoolhouse I had imagined. To the side of the school was the football field where several players were already gathered, warming up.

Jessica turned in on two wheels and came to an abrupt stop, the front wheels of the Jeep in one parking spot and the rear wheels in another. "Come on!" She hopped down and started across the pavement, madly waving at a football player who had emerged from a side door. "Hey, come here! I want you to meet someone!"

I trailed along behind.

The player came over, brushing a shock of messy brown hair out of his eyes. He held out his hand and flashed a smile. "Hey, I'm Rick."

"Hi, I'm Marissa. Um, Anderson," I said as he pumped my hand up and down.

"She and her dad came into the diner this morning. They're the ones moving into the old Anderson farm. Marissa's from St. Louis and I thought..." Jessica proceeded to tell Rick all about me.

I looked at them and rolled my eyes a little. They looked like they were plucked right out of a country song.

"I'd better go." He kissed her and then looked over at me. "Nice to meet you, Marissa."

"You, too," I mumbled as he trotted away.

Jessica whipped around and grabbed both my hands. Her cheeks were flushed. "I told you he was cute, didn't I? What type of guy do *you* go for?"

I raised my eyebrow. "I, um, really don't have a type. Smart, I guess."

Jessica giggled and pulled on my hands. "Come on." She led me through a side door into the quiet school. Orange lockers lined the hallways and a giant bobcat was painted to look like it was breaking out of the cinder block wall above the entrance to the gym. Jessica opened the glass doors to the office. "I know he's here. I saw his car in the parking lot. Mr. J, are you here?"

A stout, balding man poked his head out of the door behind the counter. "Jessica? I thought you and

your mom were going shopping today in Chillicothe?" He stood and came out of his office. "Who do
we have here? You're not the Anderson girl, are
you?" He extended his hand to me. "I'm Principal
Jameson, but most people around here call me Mr.
J." His eyes crinkled around the edges when he
smiled.

I took his hand and shook it. "Nice to meet you.
My dad and I moved here from St. Louis yesterday."

"Oh, yes, we got your file last week. Nice to meet
you. Now let us know what we can do to make you
feel welcome." He clapped me on the back with a
meaty hand. "I'll bet you're here to sign up for classes, huh? Well, let me see..." he trailed off as he
started shuffling through the stack of papers on his
secretary's desk. "I know Betty said she put your file
here somewhere."

"I'm gonna take Marissa on a tour while you're
looking for those papers, okay? We'll stop back by
before we leave."

"Good, good," Mr. Jameson said without turning
around.

Jessica rolled her eyes and motioned for me to
follow her out the door. "Nice guy. He's really fair
and pretty cool to everyone. Here's the computer
lab..." Jessica showed me all around the school, in
what ended up being a very short tour. Comprised

of about fifty or so classrooms, the high school was laid out in an L shape with a basement under one wing which dumped out into a large cafeteria. All in all, it housed about five hundred ninth, tenth, eleventh, and twelfth graders.

"Trust me; you don't want the tray lunch." Jessica led me through the labyrinth of tables in the cafeteria. "My parents always give me money to get the a la carte items. They usually have pizza, fries, hamburgers, chips. Oh, and you'll want to sit over here with us. These tables fill up fast, so we usually have someone hold a spot for all of us."

Movement outside caught my eye. I stopped walking and stared at a picnic table under a tree that was beginning to turn red and orange near the double exit doors. I shook my head. *Had someone been sitting at that table a moment ago?* "What about that table over there?"

Jessica followed my gaze. "That table?" She rolled her eyes dramatically. "The weird kids sit out there. Just stick with me, okay? Come on. We'll stop by the office and see if Mr. J found your file."

I glanced once more at the picnic table and then followed Jessica up the stairs to the office.

Mr. Jameson handed me a stack of papers and books. "Here's your schedule. The teachers have already put together some things to get you up to speed, but looking at your file, I doubt it'll be too difficult for you to catch up."

I smiled. School had always been pretty easy for me. "Thank you."

"Looking forward to seeing you on Monday morning, Marissa." He shook my hand again. "And you," he said to Jessica, "have fun shopping with your mom."

"Thanks. Bye, Mr. J." Jessica grabbed half of my stack of books and used her back to open the door. "Daddy said he'll call you about fishing next weekend."

"Fine, fine." Mr. Jameson disappeared into his office and Jessica and I headed outside.

"So, what do you think?"

I swallowed. "I don't know."

Jessica wrapped her free arm around my shoulders and squeezed. "It'll be fine. I promise."

After dumping the books in the backseat, we climbed into her Jeep and roared down the road. I leaned against the door, letting my cheek press against the cool window. As we rounded a corner, Jessica shrieked and jerked the wheel to the left to avoid a person walking on the shoulder of the road.

"What the heck?" She glanced into her rearview mirror as she gained control of the Jeep again.

I turned in my seat and looked behind us. A girl with messy black curls walked with her face down, buried in the collar of her coat. She looked up at me with cautious green eyes as we drove away.

"Hey! Who was that?"

Jessica glanced into her rearview mirror again. "Huh? Oh, that's Genevieve. Remember the weird kids I told you about? She's one of them. She actually lives about half a mile from the old Anderson farm, um, your farm I mean. I wonder what she's doing? It must be close to a seven mile walk. Her mom probably wrecked their car again. Her mom's, you know..." Jessica held an imaginary bottle in her hand and tilted it to her lips. "Oh, my favorite song!" She turned up the radio full blast and sang along.

I looked out the window again. I was certain that Genevieve was the person I saw peering in the window last night. I wasn't sure whether to feel angry, sympathetic, or just plain curious. All I knew was that I needed to talk to her and find out why she had been there.

Dad was already waiting for me as we pulled back into town. He leaned against the hood of a huge gray pickup, carefully straightening a candy wrapper between his fingers. Jessica squealed into the parking spot next to the truck and we both jumped out.

"So, are you all signed up for classes?" Dad smiled.

"Yeah," I said. "What's with the truck?"

"The Mercedes isn't going to do us any good out here. I traded her in for this. You ready to head back to the farm?" I silently thanked him for not calling it "home" yet. I wasn't ready for that.

Jessica dumped the pile of books into my arms. "See you Monday. Hey, want me to come pick you up?"

"Uh, sure."

"I'll be at your house at 7:30 then." She gave me an unexpected hug before hopping back into her car and driving away.

"She seems nice." Dad cringed as Jessica almost ran over an elderly couple trying to cross the street. "Did you get a word in edgewise at any point this morning?" He turned to open the door for me.

I climbed up into the cab of the truck. "I-don't-know-what-you-mean. I'm-perfectly-able-to-talk-a-hundred-miles-an-hour-without-the-assistance-of-any-breath-at-all. Do-you-wanna-hear-all-about-my-boyfriend-Rick-and-how-many-friends-I-have-in-cheerleading?"

"Marissa." His tone was severe, but I heard him snort as he closed my door.

CHAPTER 3

After the moving truck delivered our furniture that afternoon, it didn't take long for the house to start looking less like a scene from a horror film and more like the place I'm sure my dad remembered from his childhood. The plumber and electrician came out and by the time the sun set, we had running water, heat, *and* electricity.

As I anticipated, Dad set up his office in the room with the glass doors and moved his bedroom furniture into the room down the hall. He placed a bowl of candy on his huge mahogany desk, but I knew it wouldn't be long before bowls of butterscotches littered every flat surface in the house. I staked out the big bedroom upstairs. It had three windows that looked out over the porch roof and down onto the front yard, where trees sent bright red leaves skittering around on the grass. The room had dark brown hardwood floors that had been buffed until I could see my reflection in them and the walls were painted a pretty cinnamon color. In the corner was a huge closet. All of the furniture from my old room fit with space to spare. Dad promised I could look for some more furniture at the store next weekend.

While I unpacked boxes the next day, Dad unclogged the flue and as we relaxed on the massive sectional with peanut butter and jelly sandwiches to survey the weekend's work that night, a fire was roaring in the wood stove and football was playing on the television screen. I pulled the blanket over my feet and chewed slowly.

"So, what do you think?" Dad took a long drink of milk and wiped his upper lip with the sleeve of his flannel shirt.

I looked around and considered for a moment before answering. "I think it's going to be okay."

He was quiet for a moment. "Yeah me, too."

After a virtually sleepless night, I finally gave up trying to make my eyes close and got up before the sun. By the time I was putting the finishing touches on my makeup, trying desperately to make a straight line with my eyeliner, I heard Dad moving around downstairs. A few minutes later, he walked into my room, holding a steaming cup of coffee.

"Morning," he said.

My hands were shaking so badly I was afraid I was going to start school looking like a drunk version of Cleopatra, so I opted to go without eyeliner and put another layer of lip gloss over the three layers already on my lips. "Does this outfit look okay?" I turned back and forth in front of my mirror in a pair of faded jeans and a maroon shirt, and then swept my hair into a knot.

Dad took a sip of his coffee and looked at me. "I think you look fine," he said decidedly. He walked across the room and squinted out the window while I tossed clothing out of boxes, looking for my favorite scarf. "My mother used this room as her sewing room. She used to say the trees reminded her of fireworks in the fall."

I found my fuzzy brown scarf in the bottom of the third box I looked in and held it up triumphantly.

"Looks like your ride is here," Dad said.

I grabbed my backpack from the bed and leaned over to peek out the window. Jessica's Jeep barreled down the driveway, stopping with a skid and sending gravel skittering up to the front porch. She honked.

"See you later!" I yelled as I ran down the stairs and banged through the back door.

Jessica leaned over to unlock my door and I climbed into the passenger seat. "Are you ready for this?" She threw the Jeep in reverse and kamikazed up the driveway backwards.

I grabbed for my seatbelt and buckled in. "I don't know. I mean, I've never been the new girl before. Not to mention, I'm starting a month into the first semester."

"Don't worry. I think we have a lot of the same classes and I can help catch you up. You'll be fine." She screeched around the corner and hit the highway. "Really," she said, "you'll be good."

I found out, she was right. Being the new girl at a small school was sort of like being a celebrity. Everyone wanted to meet me and be seen with me. All through that first week of school, I was practically mobbed by girls wanting to know where I bought my clothes and boys wanting to be the first to date the novelty. It was cool for the first couple of days, but I needed a break and was already looking forward to a quiet weekend with my dad on the farm, when Jessica picked me up on Friday morning. As we drove out of the driveway, I turned to her. I had been thinking about the following conversation now for a whole week and approached it with care.

"Do you know much about Genevieve Patton?" I looked at Jessica out of the corner of my eye, trying to gauge her reaction as I reached down to grab my book out of my backpack in what I hoped looked like a nonchalant move. The truth was, I had been doing recon on Genevieve on my own ever since I realized it was she that had peered through my window the night we arrived in town. So far, I knew that she had gone to school at Culvers Grove R-II since kindergarten and her mother worked at a meat packaging plant two towns over. They lived in a trailer park down the road from our farm.

I also knew other things. Like, Genevieve kept mostly to herself and always wore at least one article of black clothing, usually with some crazy colored tights. She had long black curls that she was constantly brushing back from her face and she had an interesting combination of light green eyes and freckles. I had never seen her talk in class or the hallway. In fact, the only time Genevieve looked even remotely like the other juniors at Culvers Grove High School was when she was sitting on top of the picnic table outside the cafeteria. She smiled and talked with two other people from art class, Andy Bryant and Tristan Reynolds.

Jessica stopped the Jeep at the stop sign to turn onto the main highway. She looked warily at me for a moment before shrugging her shoulders. "What do you want to know?" She blew a huge pink bubble that popped loudly against the din of rock music pouring from the speakers. She turned on her blinker and started to pull out.

"STOP!" I stared with terror at the car that came barreling along the road toward my door. Jessica had just enough time to slam on the brakes. The car honked and swerved out of the way.

The Jeep stalled and Jessica looked over at me and smiled. "That guy came out of nowhere, huh?" She cranked the engine and the car roared to life again. My heart had not yet returned from its impromptu journey into my throat, and I gasped for air for the next few seconds.

"Must not be our day to die!" Jessica tossed her blond hair over her shoulder. As soon as the words left her mouth, she instantly looked sorry. "Oh, man, I'm sorry about saying that. I know your mom just died and stuff. I apologize. Really."

"S'ok." I leaned down to retrieve my chemistry book from the floor. The memory of my mom's face floated in front of mine for a moment.

Suddenly, I sat up, my heart beating in a panicked staccato with a singular thought. I couldn't remember which side of my mother's face had that freckle. *It was near her eye, but which one?* A tear escaped and slid down my cheek. *Was I forgetting about her?* I tried to take a breath, but my chest hurt. When she died, I thought I would never forget anything about her and now I couldn't even remember the details of her face.

"Are you sure you're okay, Marissa?" Jessica asked. "You look really sad."

"I'm okay. I realized that I need to do something." I promised myself I would look through my photo album as soon as I got home and memorize Mom's face. I also decided to write down one thing a day that I remembered about her because I never wanted to forget anything about her again.

"She's a loner." Jessica leaned over to turn down the volume on the radio.

"Huh?"

"A loner. Genevieve Patton. She makes good grades, is in choir and art, and she's a loner."

Great. Most of this was information I had gleaned on my own. What I really wanted to know, what had been keeping me up late at night was why on earth had she been looking in my window that night? "Is that all?"

"Why the sudden interest in that creepy girl?"

"Why do you say creepy?" I countered.

"Well, there's a rumor around school that she's into..." Jessica's voice dropped low, "...Satanism!" She glanced over, waiting for a reaction. When I failed to produce one, she said, "Didn't you hear me? I said she worshipped the devil."

"I heard you. I just don't think it's true."

"And how would you know?"

"We had all sorts of kids at my school that looked and acted like Genevieve. Just because she wears black, doesn't mean she worships the devil." I glanced over.

Jessica stared sullenly out the front window.

I shook my head. "I'm sorry. I meant that maybe Genevieve isn't all that bad, you know?"

"All I know is what Mom and Daddy say about her family and if you're smart, you'll steer clear of that white trash mess." She glanced over at me. "I mean it, Marissa. She's bad news."

"Fine, I'll leave it alone." *For now.* I tucked away the rest of my questions about Genevieve for the moment. I tried to concentrate on my chemistry book, but Jessica's silence was deafening. She was quiet the rest of the way to school.

"Are we okay?" I asked her as we made our way to the front doors.

She looked over at me. "Yeah, we're fine." Rick met her at the door and she threw her arms around his neck. He kissed her and she said, "Look for me at lunch!" as I passed by to go to zero hour.

After the morning of classes, I headed to lunch. Trotting along the hallway, I stopped to throw my books into my locker before heading to the cafeteria. I craned my neck to the line ahead. *Where was she?* I finally caught sight of Genevieve about seven people up and let out the breath I'd been holding. She bought a small soda and went outside, pulling her jacket closer around her with her free hand. She climbed onto the top of the picnic table, her neon green leggings almost glowing in the sun. I paid for my bottle of water and apple, and took a deep breath.

Time seemed to stand still as I walked past Jessica and her cheerleader friends. They looked up as I passed and I thought I saw Jessica shake her head. I pushed open the outside door, half-expecting Genevieve and her friends to ask me to go back inside, when they stopped talking and looked up at me. Instead, Genevieve smiled and motioned me over. I sat down and took a nervous bite of my apple.

"You know Andy and Tristan?" Genevieve asked.

"Yeah, I've seen them around."

"Anyway," Genevieve said, "back to what I was saying about this weekend's sacrifice of the cow. We must offer it to the Dark Lord at exactly the witching hour."

Oh. My. God.

I had enough time to almost choke on my apple in panic before Genevieve smiled and reached over to punch me lightly in the arm. Andy and Tristan snickered from their spots on the bench.

"I figured you'd heard the rumors," Genevieve said. Her chin ticked up a notch. "So, St. Louis, what are you doing at our table? You know you're never going to get a date now that you've been seen with us, right?"

"You were in with the cheerleaders," Andy said wistfully around a gigantic mouthful of cheeseburger.

"Easy, Tiger." Tristan rolled his eyes and held out his hand. "I'm Tristan and this is Andy."

I took his hand and shook it. "Nice to meet you both."

Andy nodded his head in my direction. "You're the one who lost her mom, right?"

Tristan closed his eyes for a moment. "I am so sorry. Andy's not the best with, you know, the people skills. We're really sorry to hear about your mom, Marissa."

I swallowed. "Thanks." And, then I waited for it. The uncomfortable silence where no one made eye contact.

"How's the old farmhouse treating you guys?" Tristan asked without missing a beat.

I smiled inwardly with relief. "Um, it's fine. We got everything moved in last weekend. Dad and I were going to go to Chillicothe tomorrow to pick up a few more things."

"You should go to Midwest Furniture. They have a decent selection." Tristan grabbed his backpack off the table and stood up. "It's where my parents got their dining room set."

"Thanks."

"See you later." Tristan headed through the doors into the cafeteria.

I stood up and looked at Genevieve. "I wanted to ask you about something," I said. "You have a minute?"

The bell rang and the students inside scattered like cockroaches.

"Sure." Genevieve grabbed my apple and took a bite of it as she jumped off the picnic table. She opened the door for me and waved to Andy. "What's your next class?"

"History."

"Me, too. Come on. Mrs. Shaull's a total crazy person about tardiness."

We wound our way through the crowded hall. I stopped by my locker to grab the ancient tome we had to use for History class.

Genevieve leaned up against the bank of lockers. "Your name's Marissa, right?"

"And you're Genevieve." I slammed my locker closed and we started down the hallway again.

"Ugh, yeah, Genevieve Victoria Patton at your service." She drew herself up and bowed ceremoniously, causing two football players to almost trip right over her. They walked away mumbling something about weirdos at the school. "My mom named me that because she thought it sounded...glamorous," she breathed out in a whisper. "Me? I think it sounds like a stripper down on her luck in Vegas. You can call me Evie. That's what all my friends, well, Andy and Tristan anyway, call me."

I stopped and faced her in the hallway, people rushing past on either side. "Why were you peeking through our window the night we moved in?"

A flush rose to her cheeks and she chewed on a thumbnail nervously. "I didn't think you saw me."

"Uh, yeah, you scared the crap out of me! What were you doing?"

"The farm's been empty for a while now and well..." she trailed off.

"What?"

"This is going to sound stupid." Her eyes dropped to the ground.

"Stupider than scaring someone who just moved into town?" I countered.

She looked back up at me. "Fair. All right, when your grandparents passed away, the old place looked...lonely."

"Lonely?"

"Don't you believe places can feel?" She leaned close. "Don't you think they hold memories like people do? I think that when your grandparents left, something inside that place that had been filled up with so much life mourned for them. And, so, I kept an eye on it."

"What do you mean 'kept an eye'?" The halls had gradually cleared out and I became aware that we were alone in the corridor.

Evie shifted from one foot to the other. "I told you it was stupid." She started to walk away.

"No, stop!" I grabbed her shoulder. "I didn't say it was stupid. I want to know more about it. I believe you. I believe things can hold onto memories. Keep going."

Evie sized me up for a minute, and after a second, nodded. "Fine. I started visiting the farm a lot to sort of keep it company. I took care of the outside, tearing up weeds in the flowerbeds, pulling vines off the sides of the barn, keeping it looking the best I could. When I saw car lights heading down the driveway that night, I wanted to see who it was. I never meant to scare you, honest!"

"Then, why did you run away when you saw us? That doesn't help the creepiness factor much."

"I don't know. I guess I didn't want you to think I was weird like everyone else does at this school. I thought maybe I'd have a clean slate with you, you know?" She looked down and swept a hand through her hair.

"Listen, Evie, I'm not mad, and I don't think you're weird. And, really, if you miss the place, you can visit it anytime. Just don't peek through the windows. Come up and ring the doorbell like a normal person, okay?"

Evie looked up warily and her face broke into a slight grin.

"Miss Patton!" A sharp voice rang out behind me. Mr. Blythe was standing in his doorway glaring at us. "Get to class immediately. This is not social hour!"

With a giggle, we dashed down the hallway and up a flight of stairs. We waited at the doorway for a moment until batty old Mrs. Shaull turned her back and then we dove for our desks, opening our books with a triumphant grin.

"Ladies, I'll see you in detention tonight," Mrs. Shaull said over her shoulder as she began writing on the board.

CHAPTER 4

Dad didn't say much on the way home. I sat in the middle of the truck seat, looking out the windshield at the fields and trees streaming past. Evie was appropriately pensive in her spot next to the door, her earlier attempt to goad my dad into a conversation proving unsuccessful. Only after we turned off the main highway did my dad speak.

"First week of school and I'm picking you up from detention? Marissa, you never got into trouble in St. Louis. Is this going to be a pattern of behavior I can expect?" He glanced over at me, the setting sun highlighting his tired blue eyes.

"Dad, it was just a tardy. It's really not that big a deal. Really!"

"Well, that's where you're wrong. It *is* a big deal. Getting a call from the principal saying my daughter's received a detention during her first week at a new school is not how I wanted to start my weekend!" He glanced over at Evie. "Now, Genevieve, dear, where do I turn off to take you home?"

"Right up here on the left," said a small voice from my right. "It's the third trailer on that side of the road."

My dad turned the wheel and the truck cruised past a weathered sign that read "Chariton Heights Mobile Home Park" in faded black letters. A vine with scraggly leaves clung to the sign and a stray cat stared out at them with baleful eyes before darting away as Dad turned into Evie's driveway.

She was out of the truck before he could turn off the engine. "Thanks again, Mr. Anderson. Sorry, Marissa. I'll see you on Monday."

"Don't you think I should walk you in and talk to your mother?" Dad rolled down the window.

"It's okay. She works the swing shift at the plant, so she's probably already gone. I'll talk to her tomorrow morning." Evie stepped back slowly from the truck. She bounded up the wobbly cinder block stairs and yanked repeatedly at the screen door until it popped open, almost knocking her off the small stoop. She waved, smiled, and then disappeared into the trailer.

My dad waited a moment, seeming to make up his mind about something and then he backed out of the driveway.

"Really, I am sorry," I said as we pulled up to the farmhouse a few minutes later. "But you know, statistics show that one out of every twenty of the nation's students serve at least one detention in their high school careers." I attempted a smile at my dad, but his scowl made me blurt out, "I promise it will never ever happen again!"

Later that night, I was reading at my desk when Dad knocked on my door.

"You should get to bed early," he said in a tone that let me know that the afternoon's infraction had already been forgiven. "Don't forget we're going to Chillicothe for furniture tomorrow."

Before knowing the words were actually leaving my mouth, I asked, "Can Evie come with us, too? Her mom's going to be sleeping all day and she doesn't have her own car and she told me she doesn't have a lot of friends and -"

My dad held up a hand and laughed. "Whoa, there!" He rubbed the stubble on his chin, the scratching noise carrying in the quiet house. "I don't care as long as it's okay with her parents. Listen, I'm sorry I came down on you so hard. I know moving here hasn't been easy for you." He rubbed his hand over his eyes and leaned against the doorjamb. "Are you acting out because you're mad at me?"

I pushed my chair back from my desk. "Okay, first of all, it was one detention for getting to class late. I'm not acting out of anger or teenage angst or any of that. It was a mistake and I won't make it again. As for moving here," I paused, "I understand why you had to do it. I mean, every place I went in the house in St. Louis reminded me of her. And it hurt. All the time." I could hear my voice hitching. I took a deep breath and went on. "I know that this was the only choice for us. I'll try my best to fit in here. It will be okay. I promise."

He nodded and sipped his coffee. "All right then. Night."

"Night."

After Dad closed my door again, I pulled out my phone and texted Evie. *Dad and I are going to Chillicothe tomorrow morning. Want to come?*

The response was quick: *Sure!*

Pick you up at 7.

A.M.??? Then, *ugh.*

I put my phone on the charger and went to take a shower. The bathroom was located between my bedroom and the room we were using for storage on the back of the upper story. The water took forever to get hot and I brushed my teeth while I waited. When steam began pouring out from over the shower curtain, I climbed in and let the water run over my hair. I hummed a song while I shampooed.

The door opened and closed.

"Dad?" I squinted one eye open.

No answer.

I looked down as gooseflesh rose up along my arms despite the scalding water pelting down on me. I already knew there wouldn't be anyone in the bathroom if I pulled the curtain back, but I couldn't resist doing it anyway. I peeked around the curtain and saw my own reflection in the foggy mirror above the sink. No one was there. I sighed and went back to my shower. I shook my head. I was tired, and stressed. After my shower, I climbed into bed and fell into a dreamless sleep.

The next day, Dad and I picked Evie up and headed down the highway. Evie and I chatted about school and Dad listened to talk radio stations he could find along the way. We got to Chillicothe and Dad stopped to ask for directions to the furniture store when he filled up at a gas station on the outskirts of town.

"Pick out a futon and rug for your room. I'm going to look for a couple of chairs for the office." Dad wandered down into the gigantic showroom.

Evie and I headed over to the futons. After finding one that would tuck perfectly under my windows along the front wall of my bedroom, we went to look at the rugs hanging from bars suspended from the ceiling. I found one pretty quickly. It was plush and the perfect chocolate color to go with the new paisley turquoise comforter I picked out before we moved.

Evie leaned her head around the rug to look at the price tag attached to the backing. A low whistle escaped her lips. "Didn't know I was hanging out with the Kardashians."

I cocked my head to the side. "It's not that much." My tone was defensive. I didn't know much about my parents' finances, but I did know that even after insurance, paying for my mom's hospital bills was going to take my dad years. I rubbed my hand over the soft carpet.

The salesperson came over. "Did you find one that you like?"

I swallowed. "Yeah." I pointed to a brown one towards the back marked *CLEARANCE*. "I'll take that one."

It took about fifteen minutes to exhaust everything possible to do in the furniture store, so we tracked down Dad and asked if we could look around the town. With a strict time limit of one hour, we scurried out of the store and down the sidewalk. A vintage clothing store caught our attention for a few minutes and then we headed past a tattoo parlor and a home decorating store before coming to the Purple Unicorn Bookstore. Books were stacked up against the window and the sign out front said 50% OFF ALL USED BOOKS written in chalk.

"Oh, let's go in here!" Evie ducked through the door.

I followed her in. It took a moment for my eyes to adjust to the dim lighting. A counter hugged the wall to my left and behind it sat a man roughly the age of Methuselah. His gnarled fingers leafed through a stack of papers as he stared over his half-moon glasses at me. I smiled and waved a hand in greeting. He eyed me for another moment before turning his gaze back down to the counter.

I looked around for Evie, but she had already disappeared into the catacombs. The shelves of books rose above my head, the space between the tops of the shelves and the ceiling crammed with paperbacks laid like brickwork. I ran a hand along the spines of a section of westerns and then followed the handwritten signs to the true crime section. Pulling a book from the shelf, I thumbed through the first chapter, fine dust rising from the top of the pages as I did so. I sneezed.

Placing the book back on the shelf, I walked to the end of the aisle and headed toward the back of the store, away from the hawk-like eyes of the man behind the counter. I passed a precariously stacked pile of books, my hip grazing it. I held my breath as it teetered for a moment before steadying. A doorway led to a room filled with shelves upon shelves of paperback romance novels. Piper would have been in heaven. So far, she hadn't answered any of my texts. *She was probably busy with school.* The stabbing sadness that accompanied the thought of my friend was unexpected and I took a deep breath before winding my way through that room to another room in the very back of the store. Evie was sitting in the corner, cross-legged on a worn carpet surrounded by a pile of tattered books. She had a large book open on her lap and she was bent over it, hair brushing the pages as she read.

"Hey." I walked over. "What's that?"

Evie looked up and focused on my face for a moment. She clapped the book closed and put it to her side. "Did you find anything?"

I reached over her and picked up the book. The cover was leather-bound and frayed along the edges. "North American Hauntings," I read softly, tracing a finger over each of the inlayed words. I handed her the book and she wiped the dust from the cover.

Evie considered me with guarded green eyes. "Do you believe in ghosts?"

I thought for a minute, gauging my answer. Taking a deep breath, I sat down on the carpet beside her. "Yes, I believe in ghosts. You?"

"Yeah. My mom thinks I'm crazy, but I've experienced some things that make me believe, you know?"

"Like what?"

"Well, you know Andy and Tristan?"

"Yeah."

"We go on ghost hunts sometimes," Evie said quietly, then rushed on with, "but we've only been to a couple of places and we haven't found much."

"Ghost *hunts*?" I asked. "Like, you try to catch them?"

"Well, sort of," Evie said, "except you don't really catch them. You just look for proof that they're there. We try to find evidence."

"Have you ever found any...evidence?"

"Once." Evie paused and looked at me uncertainly. "Promise not to laugh, okay?"

"I promise." I pulled my legs up to my chest and rested my chin on my knees.

"Well, one night, we were playing around in Tristan's basement and trying out a new recorder app and when we listened to the recording later, we heard footsteps."

"Footsteps?"

"Yeah, like heavy boots walking on the wood floor above us." She stared at me.

I shrugged. "I mean, that's strange, but couldn't it have been someone actually walking upstairs?"

"Tristan's whole house is carpeted and we were the only ones there."

"Oh." I sat still for a minute. "Have you been anywhere else?"

"Not yet," Evie looked down at the book in her lap, "but this book has a lot of places that are supposedly haunted. It even has a chapter about Culvers Grove. See?" She leafed through the torn pages until she found a small entry in the chapter about Missouri. "Most of it's here," she said, lifting up the ripped edge of the page, "but it's missing this part."

My phone beeped in my pocket and I pulled it out.

My dad. *Where are you?*

"Crap! Evie, we were supposed to meet my dad ten minutes ago!" I texted back as we quickly wound our way through the bookshelves to the front counter. Pulling a wad of crumpled dollar bills from her pocket, Evie stopped to pay for the book. The old man counted it with agonizing slowness as I stood, my hand on the door and my leg bouncing.

"You're ten short." He slid the pile of bills back at her and started to put the book under the counter.

"Here," I said, pulling my wallet out of my purse. I plunked a crisp ten on the counter and grabbed Evie's arm. "Let's go."

She took the book from him and followed me out the door. "Wait!" She turned back before the door closed. "Why is this called the Purple Unicorn?"

The man's milky eyes turned to us, and he grinned, revealing crooked teeth. "Well, you've never heard of a yellow one, now have you?" His cackling followed us as we walked away.

A block later, Evie cast a glance my way. "Thanks," she mumbled into the top of the book. She held it against her chest, her arms wrapped tightly around it.

"For what?"

"I don't need your charity, St. Louis."

I stepped in front of her and stopped. "Oh, should I cancel the telethon then?"

Evie's eyes met mine and her face went through a dozen emotions so quickly it was almost funny. I started walking again and Evie caught up with me and bumped my side. A smile turned the corners of her lips.

"It's not charity. It's friendship. Besides," I bumped her back, "now the book's half mine."

Another block and my dad came into view. He was leaning against the side of the tightly packed truck.

"He looks mad." Evie's step quickened next to me.

I squinted. "Nah, he's not mad. Probably just ready to head back."

He turned as our shoes pounded up the sidewalk. "You two are making quite a habit of being late. We need to head back. They're calling for rain." He opened the passenger door of the truck for us.

I raised my eyebrows at Evie. She smiled.

On the way home, we stopped at a diner, parking the truck in a spot right in front of the window so we could keep an eye on the furniture in the back. Dad ordered eggs, bacon, and grits and Evie and I split a club sandwich and French fries. The sky turned gray and the clouds hung low. Dad glanced out the window several times while we ate, and when we left the restaurant, he stopped by a lawn and garden store to pick up a tarp. We spent almost half an hour tying it down over the furniture and then we were back on the road, the heavy clouds chasing us all the way to Culvers Grove.

Somehow, the rain held off until we got the furniture unloaded onto the covered back porch and then, as Dad was locking the truck, the skies opened up and rain pounded the dry ground around him in an icy deluge. He ran across the yard and up the stairs, but it was too late. He was drenched. He stood dripping on the back porch, his hair slicked against his head.

"Nice look." I turned to go in the kitchen.

"But, Marissa, don't you want a hug?" Dad opened his arms wide.

I put my hand on the door handle. "Um, that would be a hard no."

"Come on, Marissa. Give your old dad a hug." He grabbed me, wrapping me in a soaking wet bear hug.

"Get off me!" I yelled, the frigid water from his hair dripping on my neck.

He let go and looked over at Evie. He motioned at the door. "Come on, kiddo. We'll wait for the rain to stop and then we'll take you home."

I followed them into the mudroom and Dad took his jacket off and tossed it down the basement steps. It landed with a sloshing plop on the concrete floor. He closed the door and pulled his shoes off while I grabbed a couple sodas from the fridge. I handed one to Evie.

"If it's okay with you, Mr. Anderson, I'll stay and help move in the furniture." Evie snapped open her can. "I mean, if you want."

Dad cast a meaningful glance my way.

I smiled and nodded.

"Well, that's fine with me. We could certainly use the help."

We spent the afternoon carrying in furniture, and by the time we climbed in the truck to take Evie home, it was nearly dark. The rain had finally stopped, but the air felt heavy with a cold dampness and lightning lit up the sky above the trees. As Dad pulled up to her trailer, we could see several cars parked haphazardly in the driveway and along the street. Lights were on inside and loud music pounded from the open door. Several people stood around, beers in hand, scattered in the yard.

"See you at school," Evie whispered, never taking her eyes off the trailer. "Thanks for lunch, Mr. Anderson." She got out and shut the door. Her back was stiff as she walked through the crowd of people bathed in the headlights.

The screen door of Evie's trailer banged open and a huge bear of a man came stumbling out into the yard. The nametag sewn into his gray shirt said

GREG and his hairy belly hung out over his jeans. Following right behind was a skinny woman in a short skirt with bright red nail polished talons clutching a cigarette and a bottle of beer. She jumped onto the man's back and they both tumbled down into the yard, narrowly missing Evie as she scurried past them and into the trailer. The man and woman started screaming at each other and the people in the yard moved into a wide arc around the fighting couple. Evie's mortified face stared out at the scene through the cracked front door glass. I looked over at my dad. His jaw was set and he was rolling a candy between his fingers.

"Dad?"

"Stay in the truck and lock the doors." He opened his door and swung down to the ground.

The woman yelled at the man and he threw his beer can at her feet and then stalked off on staggering legs. Dad walked up to the woman and pointed at the front door of the trailer. I couldn't hear what he was saying, but the woman nodded and Dad climbed the stairs to the trailer. A minute later, he walked out with Evie. She was clutching a duffel bag to her chest and Dad's arm was around her shoulders. He opened the truck door and shuffled Evie in.

"We'll bring her back tomorrow afternoon, Ms. Patton," he called before putting the truck in gear and backing out. We left the trailer park in silence and no one said a word as we pulled into our own driveway. "You girls go on upstairs. I'm going to stand out here for a bit."

Evie looked at my dad and opened her mouth as if she was going to say something but then closed it and followed me into the house. I walked upstairs and showed her where the towels were to take a shower and how to turn the faucet so you weren't pounded with cold water. She shut the door and I heard the water turn on.

I walked to my room and sat down on my bed, staring blankly at the wall. *What was I going to say to Evie when she came out of the bathroom?* I held my breath and thought of my own mom. She had always volunteered as a room mother, had snacks waiting for me in the afternoon, and took me school clothes shopping. I doubted Evie's mom had ever done any of that for her daughter. I sighed and pulled my knees up to my chest.

I was still sitting that way when Evie came out of the bathroom in pink pajama pants and a Van Halen T-shirt at least two sizes too big for her. I couldn't tell from the water dripping down from her wet hair, but I thought she had been crying.

"So, I'm super glad you met my mom." Evie attempted a small smile.

"Was that your dad?"

Evie feigned a faint. "Good Lord, St. Louis! That's Greg. He's big and dumb and drunk. He'll be gone by the end of the month." Her voice dropped. "She never keeps any of them around very long."

"I'm sorry," I mumbled.

Evie sat down on the floor and wrung her hair out into a towel. "It's okay. She'll be fine by tomorrow. Can you tell your dad thanks for me?"

"Listen, Evie..." I started and then faded off. Uncomfortable silence filled my room.

"Yeah, I know."

I cleared my throat. "I'll tell him."

She smiled again. This time it reached all the way to her eyes and they sparkled. "And promise you'll let me know if he ever wants to start dating? I could set him up with my mom, the Wonder Drunk." She was back. She wiped at her eyes and tossed the towel on the back of the desk chair. "So, you wanna look at that book we got today?"

I settled down next to her on the new carpet and turned on my bedside lamp. It made a small circle of light on the floor. Evie pushed the pages of the book under the light and began to read aloud:

"The Mystery of the Weeping Bridge. The Myrtle Bridge, or as it is known to some, the Weeping

Bridge, is the site of a tragedy. People claim to be able to hear a woman weeping when they cross the bridge under a full moon."

Evie looked up at me. I shivered.

"*Culvers Grove is a quaint farming town near the Iowa border in central Missouri that boasts a ghost story of epic proportions. Members of the Ioway tribe first settled the area, but by the early 1800s, their numbers had been decimated by smallpox, war with tribes to the north, and starvation. Members of the tribe insisted that the area was cursed and they ceded the remaining land to the US government before relocating to Kansas and Nebraska. In 1823, shortly after the state's entry into the union, Culvers Grove was founded by Justin Douglas who named the town for his British-born wife Eliza's affinity for her childhood memories of turtledoves in her family's gardens. The town quickly expanded, finding a toehold in both farming and the booming fur trade.*

By 1862, the state was embroiled in the Civil War, and Justin and Eliza's grandson, Thaddeus Douglas, had just finished construction on a home for his new wife, Mary, when he was called to serve in the Union forces. He rode away from his loveless marriage as the last nail was driven in on his misguided attempt to win her affections. Shortly after, the Battle of Pea Ridge left Mary Douglas a widow and the confederate resistance in the state at the mercy of the Federal occupation. Union soldiers moved into the small town and the area surrounding it.

One early April evening, Mary was cooking dinner for herself when she heard a knock at the door. She was not expecting company, and so, with trepidation, Mary opened the door. On her porch, she found a barefoot man dressed in the torn gray uniform of the Confederacy. She was prepared to close the door when he stepped forward and then collapsed. Pulling him inside to avoid detection by any union soldiers, she was able to revive him with some smelling salts, whereupon he told her that his name was Matthias Stratford. He had also fought at Pea Ridge and his father had been killed there. When Matthias escaped from prison in Illinois, he had followed General Thomas in order to exact revenge on him for his father's death. He thanked her for her kindness then stood up to be on his way.

The aroma of dinner wafted out from the kitchen and Mary took pity on the soldier. She asked him to stay for a hot meal before he went on his way and he gratefully accepted her generosity, his blue eyes glistening with appreciation. She offered him a place to stay for the night to rest. He agreed, with the stipulation that he was able to repay her by taking *care of things around the homestead. The next evening, she offered the same and for many evenings after that, Matthias stayed at her house, wearing her late husband's clothes, eating the food she prepared for him, and soon sleeping in her bed, for Mary had found in this lonely soldier a love deeper than she thought possible. And, Matthias grew to love her back.*

But, their love was not meant to last.

While repairing the front fence one day, Matthias was spotted by the township's marshal and the next day, a posse of Union soldiers, led by General Thomas himself, knocked on Mary's door and searched her house, eventually finding Matthias hidden in the upstairs bedroom. He was taken in as a spy, and in a cruel twist, since he was no longer wearing a uniform, he was not afforded the rights of a soldier. The punishment for a civilian spy was death. Matthias was immediately taken to Myrtle Bridge and hung in a tree over the swollen creek. His secret lover, Mary, hidden in the woods, sobbed as she watched his body swing limply above the rushing water. Upon the soldiers' departure, she ran to the bridge and..."

Evie trailed off and looked up at me with wide eyes.

"And what?" I whispered.

"It doesn't say. See here? The page has been ripped. There's nothing else."

We both jumped when my dad knocked on the door.

"Lights out, ladies. We have a big day tomorrow. You two are helping me clean out the barn!"

CHAPTER 5

Dad was true to his word, and we were up with the sun. By late morning, even with the chill outside, we were all soaked through with sweat. At lunchtime, Dad fixed bologna sandwiches and orange juice to drink. We sat in silence while we munched, happy to give our sore muscles a rest.

My dad finished his orange juice and nodded to show that he had made up his mind about something. "Genevieve, I told your mom I would have you home this afternoon, so if you're ready?"

"No problem. Thanks for letting me stay last night. It's not usually like that at my house..." she

trailed off as she bounded up the stairs. The floorboards creaked above me while I threw away the paper plates and put the glasses in the sink.

"You want to come with us?" Dad tossed his
jacket on. "I have to run into town to pick some
things up after I drop her off."

"If it's okay with you, I'll stay here. I have some
homework."

"You won't be scared, will you?" He ruffled my
hair and smiled.

"As long as you're home before dark," I said earnestly. As comfortable as I felt in the old farmhouse,
I still wasn't used to all of the noises it made at
night, and it was very comforting to hear my dad
bustling around downstairs after the sun set. I
wasn't ready yet to be all alone out here in the middle of nowhere.

I waved out the front window as Evie and my dad
headed out the driveway and then washed the
glasses and wiped the table. After throwing a load
of laundry in the dryer, I trudged upstairs and took
a shower, letting the hot water pelt my sore muscles.
We had moved in all of the furniture and cleaned
out the tack room in the barn. Dad said he planned
to get to the loft this week. He had finally secured a
hired hand to help around the farm. Grant was the

son of Mr. Hoffman, the man who owned the hardware store in town.

Evie's eyes had widened when I told her he would be working here. "He's really cute, Marissa!" she whispered. "He graduated last summer and he's going to community college in Trenton. I think he was dating a girl from Kirksville, but they broke up a few months ago."

Thinking about Evie made me smile. Back in St. Louis, I used to have a lot of friends, but when our family went through my mother's sickness and death, people drifted away. They either didn't know what to say, or they were afraid of saying the wrong thing, and suddenly, I found myself very cut off from it all. I realized at some point, my life had ground to a stop and I was living in slow motion, while their lives were still going on. By the time we left, not even Piper had called to say goodbye.

Wiping angrily at my eyes, I sat down at my desk, flipping on the light. I pulled down a journal from the shelf. The cover was emblazoned with photos of kittens, but it would do. I opened the cover and started writing:

Memory #1: When I was about eight years old and bored to tears with my summer vacation, Mom would send me on a treasure hunt. She hid a treasure of beads and fake jewelry somewhere in the house and then made a map for me with an "X" marking the spot. She burned the edges of the map on the gas stove to make the paper look authentic. Then, she packed a lunch for me, put it in my backpack, and kissed me on the cheek. She sent me off wishing me luck on my journey and wiping at imaginary tears with a dishtowel. I would spend hours searching for treasure among the three stories of our home, before finally uncovering the treasure and rushing to show my mom. She would laugh and hug me and tell me that I was the best adventurer in the world.

I put my pen down and stared at the page. The words started to swirl and I watched as a tear dropped on the word adventurer, smudging it. The warm pressure of a hand pressed into my right shoulder and I leaned my head toward the sensation. Like a whisper, the feeling was gone and I was alone again.

I wiped at my eyes and closed the book reverently before placing it back on the shelf above my desk. I would try to write one memory each day. That way, I would never forget my mom and all of the beautiful things she did. I smiled as I looked around my room, and I felt genuinely happy for the first time in months.

Flipping on the radio, I turned up the volume to an almost uncomfortable level in an effort to block out everything but that happy feeling. I made up my bed and pulled pillows out from the furniture store bag, placing them on the new futon under the windows. I stood back to look at my room. *Yeah, I'm going to be okay here.*

As the light of day began to fade a few hours later, I heard a car driving up the driveway. Turning off my radio and putting down the novel I had lost the last three hours in, I looked down to see a maroon car pull around back. Running downstairs, I looked out the kitchen window to see who it was. Dad stepped out of the car and motioned for me to come out. I slid into my shoes and grabbed one of his jackets hanging by the back door. Stepping out onto the screened-in porch, I yanked the long sleeves up and shrugged my shoulders.

"So, what do you think?" he asked as I walked over.

"About what?" I countered.

"About the car?"

"Did you trade in the truck now?"

Dad sighed. "Follow me here. I'll speak slowly. This is a car. You are a licensed driver." He paused. "I figured by now, you need a car to get back and forth to school in."

Realization dawned on me. "It's mine?" I breathed.

Dad smiled. "Do you like it? It's not fancy and it's got pretty high mileage, but the guy I bought it from said that they were mostly highway miles and that it had been a good car for him." He was suddenly very serious. "Now, I know you don't ask for much and God knows you certainly haven't asked for anything since your mother died, but I want you to have this, and enjoy it."

"I'll pay you back," I whispered, running my hand along the door.

"I'll let you start helping out with the insurance and gas next year. Until then, you just enjoy it. And take me to town to pick up my truck."

I got in and turned the key. The dials lit up red and white and talk radio blared from my speakers. I reached over to turn down the volume. "Can I go by Evie's to show her after I drop you off?"

Dad grunted as he folded his lanky frame into the passenger seat. "I don't see why not." He buckled the seatbelt.

After I dropped Dad off at his truck in town, I drove over to Evie's. Her eyes glinted as she looked at the car. "You know you're picking me up for school every morning now, right?"

The next morning, I couldn't get ready fast enough. My mind was so preoccupied with driving to school that I had to run back upstairs twice for things I had forgotten. After a text to Jessica to let her know that I was driving myself to school, I pecked my dad on his stubbly cheek as he sat at the kitchen table, drinking coffee in a square of sunlight spilling in through the window.

He barely looked up over his glasses to say, "Drive safe. Keep the radio down. And use your signals."

"I will! See you after school!" I whipped open the back door and almost barreled into a person standing there.

"Whoa! Sorry about that. Is Mr. Anderson here?" He flashed me a smile revealing the whitest teeth I'd ever seen. He was tall; almost a head taller than I was and his eyes were absolutely beautiful. They were light blue with flecks of green and gold when the sunlight caught them.

"Yeah. Mr. Anderson, I-I mean, my dad. He's right here." My tongue suddenly felt too big for my mouth as he flashed another brilliant smile at me and walked across the kitchen floor to shake my dad's hand.

"Right on time, Grant. Ready to get started?" Dad folded the paper he was reading and stood up, taking one last draw of coffee from his cup before grabbing his jacket and hat from the hook. "Close your mouth, honey, you'll drool on the linoleum," Dad whispered as he brushed past me.

"Bye, Grant," I muttered as he walked past.

"Bye..."

"Marissa."

"Bye, then, Marissa." Grant's cologne lingered in the kitchen around me as I watched him follow my dad across the yard. I walked down the back stairs on shaky legs and got into my new car, all the excitement returning as I turned over the engine. It took a minute for the windows to defrost, but soon, the inside was toasty warm and I was gingerly backing out of the driveway. After a quick stop to pick up Evie, we were sailing down the road, singing at the tops of our lungs. Pulling into the parking lot at school, I couldn't help but smile at the curious looks.

"Yep, take it all in, people. The new girl has a car now."

"Stay off the sidewalks, America."

"Shut it, Evie."

The morning dragged by, only made interesting by Mr. Smith's geometry class. He came in the door as the bell rang, dressed in a raincoat, rain hat, and boots for his lesson on volume and density. He then proceeded to splash away in a tub in the front of the room, drenching the entire first row.

Jessica caught up with me in the hallway, wringing water from the end of her ponytail. "So, we've decided something," she said.

"Who are we, and what did they decide?" I spun the lock on my locker.

She paused dramatically. "Rick and I have decided that we want you to come to Laura's Halloween party with us this weekend."

"Okay."

It was obviously not the reaction she was looking for. Her face fell and she suddenly became very interested in a hangnail. "Listen, I know that we're probably not as exciting as your St. Louis friends, but Laura's parties are epic around here and we want you to come along."

I felt bad. "Believe me," I rolled my eyes, "my St. Louis friends were not that exciting. I'll go. Thanks for the invite."

"Great! Rick and I will pick you up at eight on Friday night. How long can you stay out? You wanna tell your dad you're staying over at my house? I don't have a curfew and we could fix up the fold out couch for you. We usually don't dress up, but you can if you want. Do you know what you're gonna wear?" The deluge of questions continued to pour out of Jessica as we walked down the hallway toward the cafeteria.

"No thanks, my dad's pretty cool about curfew. I can drive myself if you give me directions, and I haven't dressed up for Halloween since I was six so I'll probably wear jeans. Is it okay if I bring Evie and Andy and Tristan?"

Jessica stopped dead in her tracks and sucked in her cheeks. "Listen," she pulled me over to the side of the hallway. "Marissa, people are starting to talk. I mean, honestly, what do you see in her?" Jessica's blue eyes scanned my face.

I shrugged. "We have a lot in common, I guess. We, I don't know, *fit*. Besides, I really don't care about climbing any sort of social ladder. I don't want to be rude, but Jessica, you *do* know there's a great big world out there outside of high school, don't you?"

"I know. It's, well, when you're from here, high school is bigger than anything else." Jessica looked down. "Forget it. It was stupid. Bring Evie if you want and sit with her at lunch. I've got your back." She smiled and pushed me into the cafeteria.

After I bought a water and apple, I caught up with Evie. I started out the double doors but she shook her head.

"Too cold out today," Evie said over her shoulder as she led me down the hallway. We went down the basement stairs and into the art room. Andy and Tristan were already eating lunch in the corner at a table made of four desks pushed together.

"Hey, Marissa!" they shouted together.

Tristan punched Andy in the arm. "Jinx! You owe me a cola." He laughed. "We were just talking about our plans for this weekend."

"Yeah." Andy raised his eyebrows. "We don't have any."

"You do now," I said as I sat down. "Jessica invited us to Laura's Halloween party this Friday."

Tristan rolled his eyes. "You mean, Jessica invited *you*." He pointed a French fry at me. "Thanks anyway, but we'll probably just hang out at Andy's house and play video games with his little sister. I owe her a beat down on Gladiator's Revenge." Tristan narrowed his eyes at me. "So, what's this I hear about you and Grant?"

I raised an eyebrow in Evie's direction. She wasn't paying attention, rather, she was picking at a run in her bright pink stockings. I sighed. "It seems someone might mistakenly have the idea that Grant and I are embarking upon some torrid affair rivaling the likes of Romeo and Juliet, but, that is *not* the case," I said in my most official voice. "He has simply been retained for gainful employment by my father at this time."

Andy snickered and Tristan punched him again.

"You do understand that Grant working for your father is all these two vultures can talk about, right?" Andy said around a mouthful of tater tots. "It's a good thing I don't get my feelings hurt easily." He winked.

"How long have you two been together?" I asked.

Andy and Tristan traded a cautious look.

I shook my head. "I'm sorry. Was it supposed to be a secret?"

Tristan pushed his food away. "It's not something we usually share too much."

"People talk in a small town." Andy reached out and grabbed a fry from Tristan's plate. "We've been together almost three years now, but he's leaving me for college next fall."

Tristan's face fell. "I told you that I'd wait a year."

"And I told you that was a stupid plan. Kansas City's not that far away."

Evie got up and threw away the package of her granola bar. She stopped and stared out the window. The edge of a purple bruise rose above the collar of her shirt. She caught me looking and yanked her collar to cover it. She sat back down and stared out the window.

"Are you okay?" I asked quietly when Andy and Tristan started talking to each other again.

"Let it go, St. Louis." She gathered up her books and hopped down from the table. "I was just thinking about something. Catch you guys later."

She walked out the door. I gathered my stuff and followed her, waving at Andy and Tristan as I left. "What were you thinking about?" I asked Evie when I caught up to her at her locker.

She turned to me, her eyes blazing. "About how it's not fair that your mom died and mine's still alive." She yanked her shirt collar up to her ears self-consciously as a group of people passed by.

A lump grew in my throat. "Did something happen?"

She shook her head and dropped her voice. "It's okay. She was drinking and she and her boyfriend got into it and...I should have stayed in my room."

"What happened?" My stomach churned uncomfortably.

"It's no big deal. She started yelling at me because I forgot to do the dishes and she ended up throwing a plate." Evie smiled sadly. "I guess I'm a little slow on my reflexes, because usually I can duck out of the way. This time, it caught me right in the throat."

I stared at her.

"Don't worry, St. Louis. Next time, I'll get out of the way. You know, I'm the white trash ninja!" She posed with her hands up in an *X* in front of her face. "I've got to get to class." She slammed her locker closed and headed down the hall.

I watched as she walked away, disappearing in the crowd leaving the cafeteria, my mind reeling. Evie was the best friend I had in this town and I couldn't let her get hurt. All afternoon, I thought about Evie and her mother, and by the end of the day, I had a plan.

We stood in front of my dad. He sat at his desk, looking back and forth from Evie to me. She shifted uncomfortably from foot to foot and I cleared my throat nervously.

"Why do I feel like I'm getting snowed here?" he asked, rubbing his eyes and reaching for a butter-scotch.

"You're not getting snowed, Dad. We thought it would make more sense now that I'm driving Evie to school every day."

"Yeah, Mr. A., and my mom's been working such long hours lately." Evie piped up from behind my right shoulder.

"So, I'm basically hosting a slumber party *every night?*"

I could tell my dad's resolve was floundering.

"It would only be for the week you'll be gone, and you know I'm scared to stay here by myself at night." Dad had to go to St. Louis for a deposition at his firm. They were fine with him working from home for most things, but it had been two weeks since he had left and they needed him to log some face time with his clients.

"I cook and clean, and I'm really good at ironing." Evie fixed my dad with one of her winning smiles. "And, my mom's last boyfriend said that I made the best meatloaf in the state!"

"Okay, girls, I'll give Genevieve's mom a call before I leave for St. Louis. I appreciate you offering to stay with Marissa. She's still a bit of a chicken when it comes to staying somewhere overnight alone." He smiled. "Now get out of here so I can call her mother."

We sat on the bottom two stairs, listening at the door of the office. I could hear the soft rumble of his voice as he talked to Evie's mom on the phone.

His voice got crisper as he walked past the doorway. "Well, I appreciate that, Ms. Patton. Genevieve's a joy to have here. Yeah, I'll have Marissa bring her by to pick up her clothes this afternoon.

Okay, thank you." He hung up the phone and sat down at his desk. "It's a go, you two connivers!" he shouted. "Go get Genevieve's stuff and then get back here so I can give you a hug before I leave."

Later that night, after Dad headed out, Evie and I sat on the couch, flipping through the channels on the television.

"Want some hot chocolate?" I asked.

"Sure."

I pulled myself up from the couch and padded to the kitchen in my favorite threadbare bunny slippers. Dad made fun of them every time I put them on. He told me the left one gave him the creeps.

Evie followed me and settled into a kitchen chair, folding her legs up under her and leaning her chin in her hands. "Your dad's the best."

"He's a pretty good guy." I looked up at her. "Do you know much about *your* dad?" I grabbed a couple of mugs out of a box and unwrapped them from their newspaper cocoon.

"Not really. I've never met him in person. Mom says he calls once in a while to check on me, but I don't believe her."

"Does that bother you?" I asked over my shoulder as I put the mugs in the microwave.

"It used to, but I mean, I never really knew the guy. I was still in diapers when he and my mom broke up. When I was little, though, I liked to pretend he was this ridiculously rich guy who would show up one day and take me away from everything. But," Evie looked down at the steaming cocoa I placed in front of her, "I think I've outgrown that." She poked absently at one of the marshmallows that tried to escape from her spoon.

"So, your mom has been dating Greg since your dad left?" I prodded.

"No, she's only been dating him for about a year now. Before that there was Gary, Keith, Randy, and Brent."

I looked down into my cup as I took a drink to shade my surprise.

"Yeah, I know," Evie said, smiling wryly. "Nothing like your mom being the town drunk *and* the town whore. How lucky am I?"

"Evie," I formed the question slowly, "I don't mean to pry, but if you hate her that much and she's mean to you, why do you stay around? Can't you move in with an aunt or something? Why don't you leave?"

"Because, St. Louis, she's my mom and she needs me. And, besides," Evie shrugged and sipped at her hot chocolate, "there is no one else."

CHAPTER 6

Friday afternoon, my dad got back to the farm. Evie and I helped him carry in boxes of casework that he said would keep him busy practically all winter. Evie had finally agreed to go with me to Laura's party and she went upstairs to take a shower. I wandered into Dad's office and sat down in one of the new soft leather wingback chairs, watching while he sorted through the files and placed them in piles on every available flat surface in his office.

"What are you up to tonight?" he asked absently, glancing at me over the top of his glasses as he flipped through the stack of papers in his arms.

"Jessica and her boyfriend invited us to a party at Laura's."

"Who's Laura?"

"You haven't met her. She's a girl at school."

"Senior?"

"I think so."

"You'll be careful and take care of yourself and your friends?"

"Yes."

"You won't drink? And if you do, you'll call me?"

"Yes, Dad, I'll even be home before midnight. Is it okay if Evie spends the night again?"

"Why not? She practically lives here anyway."

"Thanks."

"You know I should start charging her rent!" he called after me as I bounded up the stairs to get ready for the party. I put on a new facial mask Jessica had given me to try. It was bright green and made my cheeks tingle. While I was rolling curlers into my hair, the mask stretching my face as it dried, I heard the doorbell ring and my dad's voice. I wandered downstairs in my bathrobe to get a soda from the fridge. As I walked around the corner, I bumped right into Grant.

"Hey, there!" He took a step back and steadied me by holding my upper arms. "Going to a costume party?"

I blushed crimson under the cucumber aloe and tried to smile, the mask making that a difficult endeavor. "Yes. Well, no, um, not in this. This is my normal evening crypt keeper look. Like it?" I smiled with a confidence I didn't feel.

Grant laughed and considered me for a moment. "Not so bad, I would say. In fact, since I've seen what's under that," he motioned at my face, "I am going to tell you that I think you're the prettiest crypt keeper I've ever met!" He flashed his grin at me and blushed a bit on his own. He looked down as my dad walked into the kitchen.

"Here's your check for the week. Big date tonight, kid?" Dad clapped a heavy hand on Grant's shoulder.

Grant smiled. "I'm not seeing anyone right now. Just saving up for books next semester, but I *was* wondering, sir, if I could ask your daughter out on a date sometime."

We all three stood in the kitchen as the late afternoon sun spilled across the floor. No one said anything for a full minute. Then we all started talking at once.

After the flurry died down, three things had been decided: one, Dad was going to need Grant for at least another month on weekends to help around the farm. Two, Grant and I would be going on a date soon, and three, this would go down as one of the most mortifying moments of my life.

When Grant left, Dad turned to me, his mouth open.

"Not one word," I said over my shoulder as I climbed the stairs.

Evie couldn't stop laughing. When she got out of the shower and I told her about the incident in the kitchen, she was at least polite enough to ask a few questions before doubling over in laughter. Since then, she had alternated between giggles and snorts from the passenger seat of my car on the way to Laura's. I tried to concentrate on the dark road. The almost constant rain for the last two days made traveling on the gravel roads nearly impossible.

"Where is this place?" I strained to see in front of me. The canopy of a grove of trees created a skeleton pattern of moonlight on the road. I had gotten directions from Jessica, but as with most things she said, I felt like I had missed three or four key bits of information. We were several miles out into a maze of country back roads.

"I don't know," Evie said, stifling a last lone giggle. "I've never been to one of these. I'm a creepy art kid, remember? How about up there? See those cars?"

We pulled up to a line of several cars parked along the side of the road. Not wanting to get sucked into the wet ditch, their drivers had left little room for my car to squeeze by. I crept along, stopping to let people cross to a field on my right that led up to a brightly lit house. Evie rolled her window down and the sounds of laughter and music wafted in.

"I guess we found it," I said through gritted teeth as I attempted to parallel park my car for the first time. Several minutes later, we were trudging up the hill along with a couple of juniors I recognized from my geometry class. We barely reached the porch when I heard a squeal and saw a tangle of blond hair rushing toward me.

"You came! Rick said you wouldn't come because it was too far out, but I told him that I had given you good directions, and for Pete's sake, you could ask almost anyone in town how to get here and they would all know. I think Laura's parents had these parties when they were in high school." She paused and looked over my shoulder. "Hey, Evie."

Evie raised her hand in a noncommittal wave.

Jessica put her arm around me and led me into the house, Evie trailing behind. "Do you want something to drink? There's a keg on the back porch. Rick's back there with his football buddies and I came up to let some more people in. That's when I saw you drive up. Let's get you a drink and then we'll go down to the basement. I want you to meet Laura and some of her friends. They're downstairs shooting pool." She looked over her shoulder. "You can come, too, Evie."

"Oh, may I?" Evie muttered.

I glared at her.

Jessica grinned. "Of course you can!"

We made our way into the kitchen and I grabbed a soda from the cooler.

"Designated driver." I held up the can to show Jessica. "Evie, you can drink if you want."

"No thanks." Evie looked around. "I'm sure my mother would encourage me to take a few drinks to make this bearable, though."

"Would you smile and give this a try?" I hissed in her ear. "You said you've never been to one of these. Give it a chance, okay?"

Evie plastered on a fake smile and blew me a kiss. "Sure, but if I'm not having fun in twenty minutes, can we please go?"

"Fine."

It didn't take twenty minutes. After making the rounds through the thicket of high schoolers, we ended up in the crowded kitchen talking to a group of Rick and Jessica's football cronies. We were making small talk when Rick came barging in through the back door, shirtless and wearing a huge grin. He saw me and made a beeline, gathering me in to a bear hug that almost cracked my ribs.

Jessica pried him off. "Rick, you're such a goofball!"

Rick gave her a very sloppy kiss and then disappeared out the back door again.

Jessica wiped her mouth and smiled at us. "What am I going to do with him?"

"I don't know, but *you* may want to get a tetanus shot," Evie said under her breath.

"Follow me. I want you to meet Laura and her friends from Northwest. They came in for the weekend."

I followed Jessica, but about three steps down, a thick cloud of sweet smelling smoke engulfed us and I reached up to hold my nose. I started coughing and backed up into the kitchen. Jessica and Evie followed me.

"What's wrong?" Jessica asked.

"Allergies," I lied.

"I'm sure Laura's parents have something. Want me to look?"

"It's a special prescription." I coughed a couple of times for effect as Evie and I backed toward the door. "Sorry, Jessica, I have to go."

Jessica stood in the middle of the living room. "Feel better, okay? Do you need a ride home?"

"We're fine, thanks." I grabbed our coats from the back of the couch as we passed. I wrapped my scarf around my neck and pulled on my gloves as we walked down the hill. "It was a bad idea, okay?"

"Who knew you were such a prude, St. Louis?" Evie elbowed me.

"Not a prude, just careful." I unlocked the doors and got in, turning the heat on full blast. "I've planned to go to St. Louis University since I was old enough to walk. I want to go into medicine and I know that it only takes one mistake to ruin everything."

"I get it," said Evie as I pulled the car out onto the road. "I guess now I can say I've been to one of Laura's parties. Not all it was cracked up to be, if you ask me."

At an intersection of two winding gravel roads, I flipped my blinker on to turn the way we had come earlier.

"Hey, I know this road. Take a right here. I want to show you something." Evie nodded her head toward her window.

I switched my blinker and pulled out onto another gravel road that wound its way through trees and fields. We drove along for about ten minutes and the further we drove, the less populated and more intimidating the openness of the landscape became. The clouds encroached on the moon, blocking out its light.

"How much farther?" I said, irritated at the tremor in my voice. My mind started reeling through an emergency plan in case something happened and my car stopped or we ran off into a ditch. I took my suddenly clammy hands off the steering wheel for a moment to wipe them on my jeans. We came to the top of a hill and the clouds released their hold on the moonlight. Below, was a large open field, and smack in the middle of the area, about fifty yards from the road was a cemetery, bathed in the silvery rays of the moon. A lone tree spread its frost-tinged branches over the headstones and a faded picket fence encompassed the square of land. No houses were around and the only light I could see came from the moon. I slowed the car as we drove past and then slammed on the brakes, feeling my stomach lurch as the car slid a bit in the soft gravel before coming to a stop.

"What was that?"

"Did you see it?" Evie asked breathlessly.

"I *thought* I saw something..."

"What did you see? Pull in there." Evie pointed to a muddy path leading into the field.

"I'll get stuck."

"Not if you stay close to the road."

I gingerly eased my car onto it and turned off the engine. The stillness of the night engulfed us and I opened my eyes wide in the darkness. "I swear I saw a candle burning right on that headstone there." I pointed.

Evie turned to me. "Let's go look!" She was out of the car before I could protest.

"Evie!" I climbed out and stood by my door. "Evie, get back in the car!"

"Come on, St. Louis!"

Everything about this screamed "bad idea," but being left by myself at the car suddenly seemed much worse. Evie was almost to the fence by the time I finally got my brain to communicate to my feet that, yes, we really were going to go up there. I walked stiffly up the path, ready to run back to the car at the first hint of danger.

Evie reached the fence and walked along the outside, letting her glove trace the tops of the pickets. "Here's a gate. Let's go in and look around."

"I'm going to go with *no* here. Now come on, I promised my dad I would be home before midnight."

"And it's not even ten thirty yet! Don't be such a scaredy-cat. What's the worst that could happen?" Evie smiled at me and put her hands on the gate.

"A serial killer could find us...zombies could attack...we could fall into a grave..."

Evie laughed and gave the gate a couple of good yanks before it squeaked open on its rusty hinges. The squeaking sounded magnified in the quiet night and we both stopped for a moment and looked around. Nothing moved and we didn't hear another sound. My mind was spinning and so was my stomach. I seriously considered getting back into the car and leaving, with or without Evie, but I knew she would never leave me if the roles were reversed. Against all better judgment, I followed my friend into the cemetery.

"Where did you see it?" She made her way to the center.

I followed her, carefully avoiding stepping on any graves. "Over there," I whispered and pointed to a headstone directly behind her.

"Are you sure this is where you saw it?"

I nodded.

Evie inspected the headstone that I had pointed to. "That's what I thought. Marissa," Evie turned to me and paused for effect, "you saw the *Phantom Candle.*"

"Oh, don't say that word out here. It's creepy enough." I looked over my shoulder, my insides twisting uncomfortably.

"The Phantom Candle has been something people around here have been seeing for years. When people drive by this place, they see a candle burning on a headstone. When they stop to check it out, though, there's no sign of anything." She bent down and examined the headstone. "Nope, no wax. It doesn't feel hot. No lights around here to play tricks on your eyes." Evie seemed engrossed in her own world.

Whispers of mist floated around me, rising up to meet the outstretched limbs of the tree. I heard a shuffling sound and then a bird cried out, its call piercing my already shattered nerves. My breath hung in clouds as I stood there, terrified.

"Please, please, please, let's go." Tears stung my eyes.

"Just a minute, St. Louis. Can you read the name on this stone?" Evie knelt down. She pulled a penlight out of her pocket and shone it on the marker. "I can't quite make it out…"

Suddenly, I heard whispering close to the ground behind me. "Evie!" I yelled, jumping away from where I heard the voices.

"What?"

"I heard whispering!" I latched onto Evie's arm and pointed, feeling scared and ridiculous all at the same time.

"Awesome!" Evie shifted her attention to the spot behind us, looking absolutely thrilled with the whole situation.

Me? Well, I was a little less than thrilled. In fact, if anything else happened, I would probably have to change my pants when I got home. She pulled her phone from her pocket and placed it on the headstone near where I had heard the whispering.

"Seriously, Evie, I'm cold, I'm scared, and I don't want to be here anymore. Please, can we go?"

She smiled and put her finger to her lips. "Two more minutes," she mouthed silently. She touched the screen of her phone and started an audio recording. We waited in silence for a couple of minutes before she turned it off, putting it back in her pocket. "Ready to go?"

"Yes!" I grabbed Evie's hand and started pulling her down the path, focusing on my maroon car. The mud sucked at our feet. From somewhere behind us, we heard a branch crack. The blood pounded in my ears and my insides ran cold. Yanking Evie's arm practically out of its socket, I sprinted back to the car with her in tow. I jumped in, started the car, and locked the doors in one swift move. The headlights flooded the field and I backed out again onto the gravel road, pointing the car toward civilization.

After a little while of driving, houses and farms began dotting the sides of the road again and I felt my heart return to a somewhat normal rhythm. I wiggled my fingers on the steering wheel to encourage the blood to begin flowing to them again.

"Wanna listen?" Evie asked, breaking the silence inside the car as we turned onto the main road to town. My little car seemed happy to be on asphalt again and threw rocks and mud from the wheels onto the undercarriage as it gathered speed.

"To what?" I glanced over at her. I hadn't decided yet if I was angry with her or not.

Evie opened the app on her phone and pushed play. Static blasted through the phone's speaker.

"What exactly are we listening to?" I asked, following the road as it snaked along a bank of trees on the left.

"Okay, so I've been reading this book about ghosts and there are some people that think you can actually record a ghost's voice even if you don't hear anything while you're there. It's called an E.V.P."

"A what?"

"An electronic voice phenomenon. Listen."

"All I hear is static," I said as I pulled into town.

Evie put her finger to her lips and turned up the volume. We listened to another minute of static and then we heard it. I stomped on the brake and the car skidded to a halt in the middle of the deserted town square.

"Play that again," I whispered, sitting stock still in my seat.

She swiped at the screen and bumped the volume up to its maximum. A few seconds of static and then we heard it, a whisper so faint we almost didn't believe it.

But it was there.

"...*Marissssssa*..."

CHAPTER 7

When we arrived home, my dad was sitting in the kitchen, drinking coffee and definitely *not* waiting up for us. He smiled when we came in and folded up the newspaper he'd been reading. "Tell me about the party, girls. Was it fun?"

"It was okay," I said, my head inside the refrigerator. I scooped out two sodas and handed one to Evie. "Not really what we expected."

"We didn't stay long," Evie contributed, sitting down at the table. I hopped up onto the counter and cracked open my soda, taking a long drink.

Dad looked at the clock on the wall and back down at his newspaper. "What did you do afterwards?"

Evie and I exchanged a glance. For some reason, I decided I didn't want to tell my dad about the cemetery. I still needed time to process what had happened, and I knew he wouldn't be too happy about the idea of his teenage daughter and her friend wandering around in the middle of nowhere alone at night.

"We left early and went to grab a burger in Eagleton."

Dad nodded and took a sip of coffee. "You staying?" He looked over his glasses at Evie.

"If it's okay, Mr. Anderson. My mom's been...she's been working a lot lately." Evie looked down and started picking at her fingernail.

My dad grunted and looked back at his paper. "Goodnight, girls."

"Night, Dad." I jumped down and grabbed an orange from the counter. I leaned over to kiss him on his cheek as I walked past.

"Night, Mr. A." Evie followed me up the stairs.

"Can we listen to it again?" I tossed Evie a bag of chips from my stash.

She was perched on the edge of the bed. She pulled out her phone and played it.

"...Marissssa..."

We listened to it again three more times.

"Are you sure you didn't say anything?" I asked.

"I'm sure. Besides, the voice sounds like it was closer to my phone than we were." She tossed her phone to me. "You said you heard whispering while we were there. Why didn't I hear it? I was standing right next to you."

I turned it over and over in my hands. "I don't know. Who do you think it was?" I pulled my knees up to my chest.

Evie got up and began pacing the room, padding back and forth in her yellow fuzzy socks. "Do you have any paper?" She stopped in the middle of my room.

I pulled out a notebook and gave her a pen. "For what?"

"So I can make a list of what we want to take with us the next time we go out there. Like, we'll need a camera," Evie started writing in her scrawling handwriting.

"Wait a sec, Evie." My stomach clenched and I twisted my finger into my hair. My dad said I had done that since I was little whenever I was nervous. He told me I got so upset one night when they left me with a new babysitter that, by the time they got home from dinner, I had wrapped my finger so tightly in my hair that they had to cut it out. "I'm not sure going back is such a good idea. I really didn't like being that far out all by ourselves. Anything could happen. I mean, rural areas have a statistically higher percentage of mortality rates than cities."

Evie tapped the pen on her teeth. "So, let's see if Andy and Tristan can go with us. Would that make you feel better?"

"I guess," I shrugged. "Although I'm not sure Andy could fight anything off."

"He's skinny," she laughed, "but he's plucky. I'll text him tomorrow morning. Oh, and if we go tomorrow night, it will be Halloween, and a full moon! Can you get out of the house again?"

"That shouldn't be a problem. Since Dad got the paperwork for his case, he'll be totally tied up with that."

"Great. So, we'll take digital recorders, a camera, some flashlights..."

"...a bodyguard...a machete..."

Evie rolled her eyes. "Do you have a really good camera?"

"I have the one on my phone. Will that work?"

"Hmmm..." Evie tapped her teeth again. The sound made me cringe. "I'll have Andy go by and check one out from school tomorrow."

"No one will be there."

"No, but Andy's like the media specialist's pet project this year and she gave him a key to the supply room. She's convinced he's destined for CNN newscaster greatness and I think she believes, one day he'll say her name while he's accepting a Pulitzer." Evie held up her soda can as if it was an award. "'This is dedicated to my high school media specialist who believed in me when no one else did.'"

We fell back in gales of laughter until a thump on the floor from my dad reminded us that it was past one thirty in the morning.

"Okay, Operation Ghost Hunt commences Saturday at oh-eighteen hundred hours," Evie said as she turned off the lights.

"Goodnight, Evie," I whispered.

"Goodnight, you enormous chicken," came her response from the futon.

The next morning, when I came out of the bathroom, I found Evie sitting up on the futon, staring out the window. I wrapped my hair turban-style in a yellow towel. "Hey, do you need me to drive you home this morning?"

Evie continued to look out the window, pulling the covers up around her chin. Finally, she said, "I guess. I really need to check on her and make sure she turned on the heat last night in the trailer. She'll probably need clothes washed, too. If she even came home last night."

"You want me to stay with you?"

"No, I'll be fine. I'm going to take a shower."

"Okay. I'll be downstairs." I went to the kitchen and put cinnamon rolls in the oven. Dad had already retreated to his office and I could see him sitting at his desk in a faded flannel shirt.

He looked up when I brought the coffee pot in and refilled his cup. "Thanks, Peanut." He smiled and patted my arm. "I'm under the gun to get this deposition finished before next week so I won't be able to do anything with you this weekend. Do you and Genevieve have plans for Halloween?" His eyebrows raised hopefully.

I considered for a moment telling my dad the truth about what we were really planning, but not sure of his reaction, I decided to go with the lie. "Yeah, I think Evie, Andy, and Tristan are planning to rent some cheesy movies and watch them over at Andy's house."

"Sounds like fun," Dad mused absently, shuffling through a pile of papers precariously perched on the corner of his desk.

"Do you need anything from the grocery store?"

"No, just the normal stuff."

"Cinnamon rolls are done and I'm taking Evie home. See you later." I flitted away into the kitchen and pulled the rolls out of the oven. Evie and I both grabbed one and headed out the back door. On the way to her house, we went over the plan for that night.

"Andy's going to pick us up from your house around five or six and we'll head out to the cemetery. We should be able to get out there before it's totally dark so we can have a good look around and set things up."

"Will he be able to get the camera?" I turned onto the main road toward Evie's trailer park.

"Yeah, he said that he was heading over to school in a little while to get it. He also said that Tristan has a set of his dad's binoculars that have night vision and he'll bring those. I'll bring a couple recorders."

I snuck a glance at Evie. Her cheeks were flushed and she was smiling. "Do you really think this a good idea? I mean, what are we trying to find anyway?"

"What are we trying to find?" Evie said around a bite of cinnamon roll. She licked the icing from her fingers. "Haven't you ever had something happen that you couldn't explain?"

"No."

"Come on, St. Louis, can't you think of anything?"

"I guess." I glanced over at her again. I'd never told anyone about what happened to me. I took a deep breath. "When I was little, I was by myself playing the piano in our basement. I was trying to play this tough chord. I had tried over and over to get it right and was getting really frustrated. Before going upstairs, I decided to try it once more. While I was playing, I saw my dad lean over my shoulder, looking at the music. I played the piece perfectly and sat back, smiling. But, when I looked over to say something to my dad, no one was there."

"Wow." Evie turned in her seat toward me. "What else?"

"Nothing."

"Right. So, what I said was 'what else?'"

I glanced over at her again. She had her fingers interlaced below her chin and her eyes were wide. I furrowed my brow. "You're making fun."

She shook her head emphatically. "Not at all. I just know there's more you're not telling me."

"Fine, there was this one time at my grandma's house. My cousin and I were playing in her basement and we saw a ball of light in the corner. It was hovering above a box of Christmas decorations. When it started to float toward us, my cousin screamed and ran upstairs."

"What did you do?" Evie asked as we pulled into her driveway.

I shrugged. "I stood there. It came right up to me and floated above me and then it disappeared."

Evie gasped. "Too weird! Well, that's what I'm talking about. Don't you want to know what that was? Wouldn't it have been cool to have some proof of that?"

"I guess."

"See? We'll make a ghost hunter out of you after all. I know there's something out there, there has to be!" She gathered her bag and threw me a wink before she bounded up the concrete stoop and disappeared inside the trailer.

"I hope so," I whispered, turning the key in the ignition and backing out.

A few hours later, I was at home putting groceries away when I heard the house phone ringing. Dad's voice carried from the office as he talked to the caller and I heard him hang up.

"Who was that?" I called.

"Genevieve." Dad crossed into the kitchen and dumped his cold coffee into the sink. "She said that she needed you to come pick her up right now." He paused and looked at me sincerely. "Honey," he said,

"I don't want you going over there by yourself if you think there's something going on at her house that can hurt you. Do you want me to go with you?"

"How did she sound on the phone?" I closed the refrigerator and folded the paper grocery sack.

"She sounded like she'd been crying."

"I'll be fine." I grabbed my purse and keys. "I'll call you if I need you. Don't worry."

A few minutes later, I met Evie walking along the side of the road toward our house. I pulled over and pushed open the passenger door for her. She threw her bag in the backseat and got in, blowing on her hands to warm them up. I turned on the heat full blast and turned around in the road. White streaks of salt covered Evie's cheeks and her eyes were red-rimmed and wet. I didn't say anything while we drove to my house and neither did she. Dad was at the woodpile splitting logs when we drove up. He looked at me questioningly as Evie got out of the car and walked up the back porch steps. I shrugged at my dad and followed her into the house and up the stairs to my room.

Evie sat on the futon, staring blankly at the wall.

"Say something," I said, closing the door and crossing over to sit on the floor in front of her. "You're scaring me. Are you hurt?"

Evie took a moment to look down at me and focus on my face. "It's okay, St. Louis. My mom was her normal sweet self. I came home to find her passed out on the couch and some random guy in her bed. I told him to leave, and when she woke up and he wasn't there, she kicked me out."

"She what? She kicked you out? Y-you mean, out of the house?"

"Yeah." Evie looked at me through tear-filled eyes. "But, don't worry, she does this all the time. As soon as she needs someone to go get her cigarettes I'll be welcomed home with open arms." She rolled her eyes and swept her dark hair into a lopsided ponytail, her cheeks blazing red.

"What can I do?" I held my hands out helplessly in front of me.

"Well, you can take me to town to get a new digital recorder. Mom threw mine at me as I was leaving and I think it's in about a thousand pieces in my front yard." She smiled a smile that didn't quite reach her eyes and took a hitching breath. Her tone was somber when she spoke next. "You could also help me find my dad."

I nodded. "I promise I'll help you find him."

There was a soft knock on the door. Dad opened it and stuck his head in. "Everything all right in here?" He held a can of soda out to Evie.

She got up, crossed my room and threw her arms around my dad's middle. He looked at me over her head with surprise and wrapped her in a hug. I listened to her sobbing softly against his chest and thought of how many times I had done the same thing, and how it always made me feel better. When she had cried herself out, she backed away and looked down at the floor, sniffling. She wiped angrily at her eyes. "I'm s-sorry, Mr. A." She looked at me and shook her head. "I don't know why I did that."

"Because I don't think you've been hugged in a very long time," my dad said softly, handing her the soda can and patting her on the shoulder. "You can stay here as long as you need." He smiled and closed the door behind him as he left the room.

Evie walked over and sat down on the futon again. She tapped the top of her soda can with a fingernail. "I'm sorry. Here you take me in and I'm molesting your dad." She attempted a laugh, but it came out sounding like a strangled sob. "You know how lucky you are, don't you?"

"I do," I said quietly.

"Okay," she said, wiping away her remaining tears and drawing herself up straight. "Let's go to the store and pick up that recorder." She pulled her purse out of the bag and shrugged her coat on. "Ready?"

"I guess." My mind reeled. I didn't understand how she could switch modes that quickly, but I realized that she'd probably been doing it for a long time. The thought made me sad.

"And, let's stop and get ice cream. I feel like ice cream."

After a quick trip to the store to pick up new equipment, we headed back home with ice cream cones dripping in our laps and music blaring over the speakers. I looked over at Evie and thought that for that split second in time, my friend looked truly happy.

Later that night, I lay in my bed for a minute, listening to the ice-covered branches crackle as they blew in the wind outside my window, and enjoying the warmth of my soft bed. I could hear the shower going in the bathroom and the furnace rumbling in the basement. All of the comforting sounds made me think back to the first Christmas I remembered. I shuffled over to my desk and grabbed my notebook and pen before diving back into the cocoon of warmth under my comforter. I opened the notebook and smiled at the pages filling up with memories of my mom. Flipping through to the next blank page, I began to write:

Memory #32: Christmas was my mom's favorite holiday. Any time after Halloween was game for playing carols, putting up decorations, baking cookies and starting on the Christmas list. When I was six, it snowed buckets on Christmas Eve, and when I got up the next morning, I found piles of presents under the tree and smelled the heavy scent of strong black coffee from the kitchen. My mom said she had a surprise for me and led me to the back door of the house. Out on the lawn, there were the tracks of eight reindeer, long skids from the runners of the sleigh and big boot prints leading up to our door and then back again. It was absolute evidence that Santa had actually been at my house!

It was only when I was eleven and no longer believed in Santa that I asked my mom about it. She told me that she had gone out under cover of darkness in a housecoat and my dad's big boots. She had used a broomstick to make the hoof prints and runners and my dad's boots to make the footprints. She made me promise that, one day when I had children of my own, I would do the same for them. She told me that the look on my face when I was six that morning had been magical.

CHAPTER 8

"This is Andy Bryant and this is Tristan Reynolds. They go to school with Evie and me," I said.

"Nice to meet you Andy. Tristan." My dad took turns shaking each of their hands. "You guys want some hot chocolate before you head out?"

"No, thanks, Mr. Anderson," Tristan said.

"We're going to have snacks and cocoa while we watch videos," Evie piped up.

I raised an eyebrow in her direction and she shrugged.

"Well, have fun and I'll see you around midnight." He dropped his voice, talking only to me. "And whatever it is you're *really* doing tonight, make sure you're safe."

I nodded and gave my dad a quick hug before following the trio out the door. We drove down the road, four across the cab of Andy's truck, thankful for the warmth the tight quarters afforded us on this frigid Halloween night.

"Did you get the camera?" Evie asked from her spot by the passenger door.

"Yeah," said Andy. "It's in the toolbox in the back. You're going to have to tell me where this place is."

"I will. Keep going straight here."

Even though we had been there the night before, I was soon hopelessly lost. Evie proved to be a superb navigator, though, winding the truck through the labyrinth of gravel roads.

"So, Evie told me you've had some experiences with ghosts?" Andy glanced over at me.

Tristan turned to look at me, too. "You have?"

"I guess," I replied, "but I'm not really sure if they were ghosts, or my overactive imagination."

"Evie told us about the light in the graveyard," Tristan said. "Have you had other things happen?"

I glanced over at Evie.

She nodded.

"I don't know," I said. "Something strange happened to me about a year ago. I saw *some*thing. Maybe it wasn't a ghost, though, but, like a flash of someone." I paused. It was nice to finally be able to talk to people about all of the things that happened to me. It made them feel more real, somehow. And me, less crazy for seeing them.

"A flash of someone?" Evie asked.

I chewed on my bottom lip. "Yeah, it happened while I was outside in our backyard helping my mom plant daisies. When I looked up, I saw my mom's mom, standing at the back door with a tray. She was wearing her favorite yellow housecoat and her socks were slouching down on her legs. On the tray was a pitcher of lemonade and three glasses. I reached up to wipe the sweat out of my eyes and when I looked again, she was gone."

"Did she go back inside?" Tristan asked.

"No."

"Well, how do you know?" Andy asked. "I mean, she could have gone back in to get something."

"I know because she passed away the year before. And, I don't think she was a ghost, I think maybe she was telling me that she was okay."

"That's really amazing. Didn't your mom see anything?" Tristan asked.

"No, that's why I'm not exactly sure what it was I saw."

"That's what we want to find out when we investigate," said Tristan. "If we can find proof, then it's not just a story. There are other people there and equipment to back it all up, you know?"

"Have you guys been doing this...ghost hunting thing long?" I asked.

"Not really," Tristan said. "We've only done it a few times at our own houses. We've been to one cemetery before, but this is the first time we've been out with this much equipment." He opened a package of gum and unwrapped a piece, offering us one before putting it in the backpack at his feet. "Are you scared, Marissa? It's okay if you are."

"No. Well, yeah. I'm kind of, well, scared of everything, so I've never been brave enough to do anything like this."

"Nothing to be scared of," Andy said, "especially when you have guns like these around!" He held up a scrawny arm and made a muscle.

"Don't hurt yourself," Tristan said amid the laughter.

"There it is." Evie pointed.

Once again, we pulled up into a small flat area off the road and Andy cut the lights. Dusk was coming on quickly and we all piled out from the truck and stood looking at the cemetery. Andy began pulling things from the toolbox in the bed of his pickup and handed them to Tristan and Evie. I stood ready, but no one handed me anything.

"Can I help carry?" I asked.

"Nope," Andy quipped. "You're our sensitive tonight."

"Your what?"

"Our sensitive." Tristan laid a hand on my shoulder. "Because, what I guess we haven't told you is that while we are all really interested in ghosts, you're the only one who has actually ever, you know, *seen* one."

"Oh."

Andy threw a camera bag over his shoulder that looked to be about twelve pounds more than his own skinny frame. "So, tonight, you walk around and if you get a feeling about something, let me know, and I'll set up the equipment."

Tristan and Evie started trudging across the field to the cemetery. Andy and I hung back.

"Andy?"

"Yeah?"

"What if I don't get a...feeling? What if I get out there and I don't feel anything and we've wasted this whole trip out here and -"

"Whoa!" Andy held up a hand to cut me off. "So, this is the first big investigation we've done, okay? We really have no expectations at all for how this is going to go. Don't worry, Marissa."

I nodded.

"Come on." He started across the field and I followed a few feet behind. The setting sun cast long shadows in our wake. As we approached the gate, the trio held back while I walked up and opened it. When I stepped into the boundary of the fence, all apprehension that I wouldn't feel something immediately disappeared. Already, I felt somehow different. Spinning around in place, I tried to figure out where the feeling was coming from. A few feet away stood a large statue on a pedestal. I hadn't seen it last night. The figure at the top was dressed in long robes and its arms were outstretched. I edged forward toward it and when I was directly in front of it, a cold chill ran through me down to my toes. The figure seemed to be smirking and I reached out to touch the cold marble. My fingertips touched the lower edge of the saint's robes and my hand recoiled as if it had been burned.

"Holy crap," I whispered. I planted my feet and reached out again. This time, I forced myself to keep in contact with the statue. I was filled with a sense of icy hopelessness and I pulled away again.

"What are you doing?" Evie's voice next to my ear made me jump three and a half feet into the air.

"I think we should take some pictures of this statue when it gets dark," I said, looking at Evie earnestly. "It's off the charts for creepy."

"Yeah," she looked up at it, "I would have to agree with you on that."

We spent some time setting up, and I had to admit, I was impressed with the speed and efficiency with which Andy, Tristan, and Evie worked. They seemed like a well-oiled machine and I felt like a cog in the wheel, walking around the cemetery to figure out where we could best get photos and video and audio. When the sun had completely set, stillness settled down over the field and we were ready for whatever the night held in store for us. The tree's branches stopped moving as the breeze died down and our ears strained to hear a sound.

"I'm going to start the video feed over here," Andy whispered, indicating a place along the back of the fence. "Tristan and I will move our way up to the front near the gate. Just watch so no one gets in the shot, okay? Ready?"

They moved to the back of the cemetery, Tristan sweeping the flashlight's beam out ahead of them in a wide arc and stepping carefully around the headstones while Andy quietly narrated the video.

"Let's go this way." Evie nodded to what looked like the oldest part of the cemetery. I glanced over my shoulder at Tristan and Andy. It was reassuring to have them close, but my level of apprehension was growing in direct correlation with the darkness as the clouds obscured the full moon. Even though Evie was the one making her way closer to the awful statue, I wrapped my coat around me and shoved my hands deep in my pockets, resolved to give up my status as biggest chicken ever. *I can do this*, I told myself repeatedly in my head.

In the far corner of the cemetery, Evie approached a set of headstones that were crumbling with age. She shined her flashlight on one and read the inscription aloud, "Joseph Schmidt 1824-1910." We looked to the next one, which was in far worse shape.

"Bethany Schmidt 1827-1914. Wife and mother," I read in a whisper. Next to these two headstones were smaller ones with simple crosses on them. "These must be their children," I said quietly, the hair rising on my arms. I could see Evie shudder out of the corner of my eye. We walked along and Evie took out her recorder. She pushed the record button and the red light turned on. Setting it on the flat grainy surface of a headstone, she turned to me.

"Do you want to ask any questions?" she hissed.

"Not right now. Why don't you start and if I think of anything, I'll ask one."

"Suit yourself." Evie shrugged. "Is there anyone here who would like to speak to us tonight? My name is Evie and this is Marissa, and we are students at the high school here." She paused and we both strained our ears to hear something. "You wanna try, St. Louis?"

I took a step closer to the recorder and cleared my throat. "H-hello? Was it you I heard last night whispering? Were you trying to tell me something? Are you..." A click in front of me stopped me mid-sentence. Evie and I looked at the recorder. The red light was off.

"Hmmm," mumbled Evie, walking back over to it. "I could have sworn I pushed the button down all the way." She pushed the record button down solidly and the red light came on. She set the recorder down again and stepped back. A few seconds later, there was another click and the recorder turned off.

"Evie?" I said uneasily, ready at any moment to break and run back to the truck.

"It's okay. I'm not sure what's going on, but it's okay."

As Evie picked up the recorder, I heard a rustling near my feet. I looked down, half expecting to see dry leaves, but there was nothing and I wasn't moving a muscle. In fact, I didn't even think I was breathing at this point. The rustling came again. It sounded like someone walking through a pile of leaves in the fall. Evie stood still by the recorder, turning it over and over in her hands. I turned a bit and saw Andy and Tristan making their way along the back fence, easily one hundred feet away. The noise continued and then I heard it. A giggling sound erupted from behind me. My blood ran cold.

"Evie! Evie! Evie!" I shouted, too scared to move my feet. Andy, Tristan, and Evie were all by my side in a matter of seconds.

"What's wrong?"

"What did you see?"

"I heard giggling," I breathed.

"Cool!" Andy and Tristan said in unison.

"Yeah, cool," I said, still not daring to move.

"Where?"

I pointed to the area behind me and to my left, near the statue. Tristan came over and put his arm protectively around my shoulders, making a shushing sound that I thought was perfectly unnecessary, but appreciated nonetheless. Evie whipped out her camera and started flashing pictures with an ancient Polaroid. She handed Andy the photos and he shook them, waiting for them to develop. The moon came out from behind a cloud and bathed the cemetery in its pale white light.

Tristan grabbed the first photo out of Andy's hand and shone his flashlight on it. "Look at that," he said. We all gathered around and looked over his shoulder. In the picture was the statue with a mist rising up around its base. Tristan shone the beam of the flashlight over to the statue.

"Do you see any mist?" Evie asked.

We all shook our heads.

"Okay, keep recording," Andy said. "Marissa, do you think you can move closer to the statue and do some E.V.P. work there?"

Three pairs of eyes turned on me expectantly.

Tristan turned me toward him. "If this is too much for you, we can stop," he said quietly.

"Yeah, St. Louis. I don't want to have to pay for your therapy bill, okay?" Evie said, her smile belying the concern in her eyes.

My stomach churned and my legs felt like sponges. Every fiber of my being wanted nothing more than to run to Andy's truck and lock the doors. I swallowed. "It's okay. I'm fine," I lied. I took another step toward the statue, the whispering louder now. "Can you hear that?" I asked.

Andy shook his head.

I closed my eyes, allowing the whispering to wash over me. I began to be able to pick out words from the sound. "*...here...now...death...*"

I followed the whispering as it snaked along the ground, leading me toward the back corner of the cemetery. A huge tombstone jutted at an angle from the ground. I looked up and saw a figure standing behind it. It wavered and then became stronger. The figure solidified and my hand flew to my mouth. It was a man in a straightjacket. He took a step toward me, his mouth open and his eyes empty. "*...Marisssa!*"

"Marissa?" Evie was beside me. "You're shaking."

I turned to her. "Can we please go now?" I asked, a tear running down my cheek. I felt a sucking from somewhere inside and my eyes welled up. The cold pressed in on me and my knees buckled. I peered at her from inside a darkening tunnel and closed my eyes.

When I opened them again, we were outside the gate. Evie and Andy were struggling to walk on the uneven ground, and they were carrying me between them.

"I'm okay, guys." I put my feet down and stood up straight.

"Are you sure?" Evie asked.

"Really, I'm fine." I looked back up at the cemetery. "To be honest, I felt better as soon as I crossed
out of the gate." The feeling had come back to my
legs and I felt normal again. "I can walk by myself
the rest of the way."

As Andy was putting all of the equipment back
in the toolbox, Tristan got in the truck and cranked
the engine, bathing the forest at the edge of the field
to the left of us in bright light. I was already in the
truck next to Tristan as Evie climbed in the passenger side.

"Who's that?" I shouted and pointed out the
windshield. I saw a figure step out from behind a
tree. Before I could fully focus on it, it had disappeared. A sound wound its way from the tree line to
the truck. It was the saddest sound I'd ever heard,
a cross between crying and moaning, lilting on the
air and filling my consciousness. A chill ran up and
down my back. "Do you hear that?" I asked.

Tristan shook his head. "I don't know what you
hear, but I think it's time to go. Andy, get in the
truck!"

"Hold on a second," Andy said, his eyes never
leaving the spot near the tree. "I'm going to see what
Marissa thought she saw."

"Bad idea, bad idea, bad idea," I said, shaking
my head.

"I'll go with him." Evie climbed back down and slammed the truck door.

"Do you want me to stay here with you?" Tristan asked.

I nodded, and Tristan and I watched through the fogging windshield while Andy and Evie crept up on the edge of the forest. They walked around the tree and shined their lights deep into the woods. A minute later, they shrugged and walked back to the truck. Andy pulled out and we started down the gravel road, no one yet speaking.

"Okay, so I'll be the one to talk first," said Evie. "What did you see at the forest?"

"I-I saw a woman," I said. "She came out from behind that tree. I saw her, I thought, but then she disappeared."

After a few more minutes of silence, Evie asked, "Did you see what she was wearing?"

"It looked like," I began, "well, it looked like a long white dress." My hair stood on end and I felt goose bumps break out up and down my arms. Tristan shuddered next to me and Andy laughed nervously. We bumped along the gravel road quietly for a while, all caught up in our own thoughts as we stared out the window at the cool October night.

"Not bad for the first outing of M.E.A.T.," Andy said, breaking the silence as he turned back onto the main road. The sight of other cars driving with their lights on was comforting after the desolateness of the cemetery and the mood in the cab of the truck began to shift.

"What's M.E.A.T.?" asked Evie, leaning over to look around Tristan and me at Andy.

"Marissa, Evie, Andy, Tristan." Andy said. "We need a name. What do you think?"

We rode in silence for a minute.

"I think you're certifiable," Evie mumbled.

"You got something better?"

"Um, we could also do T.E.A.M. with the same letters," I suggested.

"How about G.H.S.? Ghost Hunters Society?" Evie said quietly.

"You tag 'em, we bag 'em!" Andy smiled.

Tristan dropped his head, squeezing the bridge of his nose with two fingers. "Stop, just stop."

"I like it," Evie said. "You guys, I really think we caught something tonight. I'm not sure what, but there was something going on there. I wish I would have heard the giggling you did." She stared at me with admiration.

"I wish you had heard it, too. Honestly, I almost wet my pants. I've never heard anything like that before."

"Do you think we caught it on the tape?" Evie asked.

"We can check it out at my house," Andy said.

After a quick run through the drive-thru because Andy insisted he was *literally* going to expire if he didn't eat a cheeseburger, he pulled into the driveway of his house. It was in the middle of town, a small bungalow that he shared with his mom, dad, and little sister. They were out trick-or-treating when we got there.

"We've got about an hour of stuff to go through here. So, who wants to do what?" Andy asked a little while later, standing in the middle of the family room in his basement. Evie and Tristan had commandeered the pizza rolls as soon as they came out of the oven, and now they were sitting on the couch fanning their tongues as they shoved the napalm hot rolls in their mouths.

I tilted my head to the side. "You know, if you let them cool..."

"Shut it, St. Louis. Starving!"

I rolled my eyes. "I guess I can listen to the audio," I offered from my perch on the ottoman. Andy threw it to me and I grabbed the recorder from the air, putting it in my lap while I started untangling the headphones.

"I'll do the video," he said. "Tristan can help me."

"That leaves the photos. Evie, are you okay with that?"

"Absolutely," said Evie, eyes flashing with anticipation.

Ten minutes later, we were all transfixed by our projects and the room had fallen quiet.

"Check this out, guys," Andy said, reaching out to pause the camera. We all crowded around the screen and he pointed to a bright ball of light near the top right corner of the picture. He hit play and we watched the ball bob along until it stopped and hovered over the statue.

"Is that a snowflake?" I asked hopefully, watching the ball dance along the screen.

"I thought it was at first," he said, "but watch what happens next."

The ball of light meandered along until it was directly over my head in the frame and then the video camera jerked as I yelled out, "Evie! Evie! Evie!" on the screen.

"Whoa," Tristan said, rocking back on his heels.

"Okay, I'm going to keep watching."

We all headed back to our jobs and continued working in silence. Evie showed Andy a couple of pictures she thought looked suspect, but they decided the white blurs were the flash bulb's reflection on dust. A few minutes later, I was listening to the tape when I heard the click of the recorder turning off. A second of silence and then Evie's voice saying she thought she had pushed the button down all the way. Another click, and then I heard a scratchy whisper. I rewound the tape and pushed the headphones tight to my ears as I listened to that part again. This time, the scratchy voice came out clear as a bell.

"*Get out...!*"

I slammed the stop button down on the recorder and stood up, doing a sort of drunk chicken dance when my feet got tangled in the rug. I pushed the recorder away and pointed at it accusingly.

"What?" asked Andy. "Did you hear something?"

"Y-yeah," I replied. "Yeah, I heard something. And you guys are crazy if you think I'm ever going back to that place again!"

CHAPTER 9

By early November, I was becoming less of a novelty and more of a normal face in the crowd at school. Most days, I wandered down the hallways waving at friends in the school that was now becoming familiar to me. I sat at the same table for lunch and had the same lab partner every day in chemistry. I wasn't sure yet how all of that made me feel, but it was nice to feel like I belonged somewhere. It was nice not to feel so displaced.

A week after the Ghost Hunters Society went on our inaugural investigation I was home eating sunflower seeds and watching television when the phone rang. I padded to the kitchen in wooly socks, picking a seed out of my teeth. "Hello?"

"Hi, Marissa? It's Grant. Sorry to call this number. I don't have your cell."

"It's fine. What's going on?" I sat down on a chair and pulled my knees up to my chest. His voice sounded a little gravelly over the phone and I resisted the urge to swoon a bit.

"Not much. I'm in Brookfield this weekend visiting my mom. Listen, do you want to go eat dinner and catch a movie with me next weekend when I get back into town?"

"Sure."

"I was thinking you could wear that green mask thing I saw you in the other night. Pretty sexy!"

"Shut up!"

He chuckled. It was a nice sound. "Okay, it's a date! See you later."

"Bye." I hung up the phone.

Did he just say "date"?

Dad headed back to St. Louis to present his deposition in the appellate court. He was planning to be back by the next night, and even though Evie had been right and her mom had invited her to move back in with her, she readily agreed to stay with me while he was gone again. That night, after Dad left, Evie and I sat upstairs in my room, listening to music and doing our homework. "This sucks!" Evie threw her book to the floor. "I can't get trig and I'll never get trig!"

"I don't think it's meant to be gotten. You have to memorize the formulas."

"Easy for you to say, Brainiac. Some of us aren't blessed with ginormous craniums like you."

"So much wrong with that sentence." I smiled and stretched, the science book I had been studying falling from my lap onto the bedspread. "Let's take a break, huh?"

Evie nodded emphatically and followed me down the stairs to the kitchen. The early November snow had been falling now for a couple of hours and we looked out the window expectantly.

"You think they'll call off school tomorrow?" I watched my breath crystallize on the glass windowpane as I spoke. "I don't see how they'll get everyone there. Most buses have to go way out in the country on gravel roads."

Evie rolled her eyes. "You are so city sometimes."

"Hot chocolate?" I asked, pulling down two mugs and the box of instant. I filled up the mugs with water and poured in the powder, stirring around the tiny marshmallow nuggets. We slipped into comfortable silence for a long time, both looking out the window at the snowflakes blanketing the yard in a sparkling layer of white.

"Marissa?"

"Uh-huh?" I wiped my lip.

"You never told me about your mom being sick. What was it like for you?"

I sighed and watched a particularly brave snowflake turn this way and that on a sharp breeze before finally disappearing among its friends on the ground. "After she did chemo and radiation, the doctors hoped that the cancer had gone away. But, three months after the treatments and surgery, they found a lump in her lungs. By the time they figured out that the cancer had spread, it had gotten into her lymph nodes. The doctors sent her home and told us that she had less than six weeks to live."

Evie sucked in a breath through her teeth.

"So, Dad and I brought her home and set her up in the living room. She always said that was her favorite room in our house. We put her hospital bed in there so she could watch us going through our day. My dad was working every day and I still had school, so she had some nurses who would come in and stay with her. They helped us with her medicine and kept her from being in too much pain." I took a breath. Part of me wanted to keep the next part private, but a bigger part of me wanted to finally tell someone. "One day, though, close to the end, I came home from school and she was lying in her bed crying. She told me it hurt and that she was ready to go. She wanted me to be ready to let her go and she told me that I...that I..." I looked up at Evie. Her figure was wavy through my tears.

"It's okay, Marissa. What did she tell you?" Evie scooted her chair around to sit next to me and put her arm around my shoulders.

"She told me I had to say I was ready for her to die. She said she wouldn't be ready to go until she knew I was ready for her to go. And I said it, Evie. I told my mom I was ready for her to die!" I felt a mixture of guilt, relief, and overwhelming sadness rush over me as the first wave of sobs hit. Evie held me while I cried and cried.

When my body felt drained, I looked up at Evie whose own eyes were red and wet.

"She passed away the next day, didn't she?"

"Yeah," I sniffed and sat up. "Yeah, she died the next day, and I feel like it's my fault. Like, if I hadn't said those words, she would have hung on a little longer."

"Well," Evie paused and stood up, looking out the window again, "that's just stupid."

I almost choked on my cocoa. "What?"

"Really, Marissa, you didn't cause your mom to die. The cancer did. And, the longer you walk around thinking that you were somehow part of that, you'll never be happy. You didn't let go of your mom. She waited until she knew you were going to be okay and then she let go." Evie turned to face me. "*She* let go, okay?"

I sat there for a while, letting Evie's words hit me full force. She was right, but if I accepted that, I also had to let go of the guilt. And, letting go of the guilt meant allowing in the anger. I wasn't sure I was ready for any of it.

"You want to go watch the news and see if they've called a snow day yet?" Evie asked, putting our empty mugs in the sink.

"Sure, and Evie?"

She stopped and turned around to face me. "Yeah?"

"Thanks."

"No worries. That's what friends are for." She smiled and flopped onto the couch, turning on the TV.

Apparently, schools didn't believe in snow days in northwest Missouri. I cursed the weather gods as I plowed through a drift up to my bumper and skidded into the parking lot of school an hour later. Peeling my fingers from the steering wheel, I followed Evie into the building, knocking snow from our boots on the already soaked carpet inside the door.

When I walked into the chemistry lab, I noticed a vase of daisies sitting on Ms. Creavy's desk. I was thinking how pretty they were and how much my mom would have loved them when Ms. Creavy pointed at me.

"These are for you." She smiled at me over the bright blue frames of her glasses.

"Oh, um, thanks," I said, turning crimson. I grabbed the vase and made a beeline for my seat, ignoring the stares from the rest of the class. Yanking the card off the vase, I ripped it open.

"Looking forward to our date Friday. I'll pick you up at 8:00. Grant."

I shoved the card back in its envelope and opened my notebook. I began to take notes, not quite sure how to deal with such an ostentatious display. When the bell rang, I gathered my books and the daisies and took a detour to my locker to drop them off. I met Evie in the art room.

"Flowers, huh?" she smiled.

"How did you hear about that already?" I glared at her. The small town high school grapevine seemed to be operating on warp speed today. "They were from Grant. He said he's looking forward to our date." I sat down and put my chin in my hands.

"Well, are you excited?" Evie asked.

"Sure I am. I, well..."

Evie motioned for me to continue. She jumped up on the counter, and smoothed her black skirt down over her purple and yellow striped leggings.

"Okay, so I've never exactly been on a date before."

She feigned surprise. "Never, Prudence McGee?"

I rolled my eyes. "Shut up. Mom and Dad said I couldn't date until I was sixteen, and when I had my birthday, Mom had gotten sick, and well...anyway, how many dates have you been on?"

Evie smiled and unwrapped a green apple lollipop. She shoved it in her mouth and made a zero with her fingers.

Just then, Andy walked in, pulling up the waistband of his perpetually sagging jeans. "What's crackin', Patton?" He sat down and took a giant bite out of his hamburger.

"How do you eat that much and stay that skinny?" Evie sighed. "I even look at a burger and I gain twelve pounds."

"Yeah, well, you aren't blessed with the metabolism of a hyperactive cheetah like me and your girl here," he laughed, elbowing me in the ribs.

"But, I have such a pretty face," Evie tilted her head to the side and fluttered her eyelashes.

"What's going on in here?" Tristan lugged his enormous backpack in the room.

"What do you carry in that thing anyway?" I asked.

"I heard you got flowers today," he deflected. "Who are they from?"

Evie spoke before I could even open my mouth. "Marissa has a big date with Grant on Friday night." She rolled her eyes back and touched her forehead with her hand, pretending to faint.

"Shut up," I growled.

"Grant? Hoffman? Didn't he graduate last year?" Tristan held a hand up to his chest. "You really don't mean *THE* Grant Hoffman, do you?"

"Yeah, he's dreamy!" Evie said from her perch on the counter.

I considered knocking her off.

"Okay," Andy said, "everybody up for hanging out Saturday night, then?"

I silently thanked Andy for not participating in teasing me about Grant.

He wiggled his eyebrows. "We can meet at Marissa's house and hear all the juicy details."

"I hope you choke on that burger." I reached out and smacked him on the back of the head as Evie and I left for American History.

"Ignore him." Tristan rolled his eyes. "See you guys later."

"Hey, Marissa," Evie said before we headed into class, "would you mind dropping me off at home tonight? Your dad's due back before dark, right?"

"Yeah, he should be home for dinner."

"Mom called school today and said she really needs me to come home."

"Are you sure you want to do that, Evie?"

"Yeah, it's usually code for me to bring her some cigarettes and do the dishes, but I need to check on her and make sure she's doing okay."

"All right, but you'll call if you need me, okay?"

"Of course," she said. "You worry too much, St. Louis!"

Later that night, I was lying in bed, listening to the icy sleet hit my window. It was really coming down in earnest now and I imagined the slick drive to school I would have in the morning. I had checked the locks at least three times each and had left lights and the television on downstairs to make it look like my dad was home. When the weather turned off bad earlier in the evening, Dad called to say he was staying in a hotel for the night in Columbia. He promised he would be home by noon the next day and I was keeping a mental countdown of the hours going on in my head. Turning over, I flipped on the television, watching the blue light flicker on the ceiling and listening to the familiar sounds of the warm house. I was surprised to find that while I didn't exactly feel at ease, at least I wasn't cowering under the bed.

Suddenly, I heard banging from downstairs. I sat up in bed, realizing I must have dozed off for a minute. I glanced over at the clock on my nightstand. The numbers 2:43 glared back at me. The banging came again from downstairs. It sounded like someone knocking at our back door. Even though I knew that statistically, most home invasions occurred during the early afternoon, I decided that perhaps the axe murderer at my back door had not received that information. I crept over to the window and saw only my car sitting in the driveway below. Sliding into my slippers and robe, I moved silently down the stairs, jumping each time a new flurry of knocks came from the back porch. Slinking around the corner and staying in the shadows, I managed to pull the phone off the set and typed in 9-1-1. My finger was getting ready to push "talk" when I heard Evie's voice.

"Marissa! Marissa, it's me, Evie!"

I made my way across the kitchen floor and flipped on the back porch light. She was standing on the back porch in a soaked T-shirt, pajama pants and socks turned black by the mud. Her wet hair hung in icy ringlets around her face.

"Oh my gosh!" I shouted, fumbling with the lock.

Evie burst through the door and fell on the floor in a sobbing, shivering pile. "I-I'm sorry," she chattered through blue lips. "I didn't know where else to go!"

In a flurry, I ran to the bathroom, grabbed two fluffy white towels and wrapped them around Evie, then led her into the living room. I threw two logs into the wood stove and she sat down on the couch in front of it. I ran back into the kitchen to flip on the coffeepot, check the lock on the back door, and grab pajamas out of the dryer. Back in the living room, I stood her up and helped her peel off her wet clothes, trying not to look at the angry red and purple bruises intermingled with older green and yellow bruises on her back and legs. My stomach turned.

After I got her dressed again and covered in a blanket, I brought her a cup of coffee with a ridiculous amount of milk and sugar in it. Perched on the edge of the overstuffed chair, I pulled a blanket over my legs and watched Evie.

We sat in silence for a while and gradually she stopped shivering. Her lips were still a nasty shade of blue and she sipped at the steaming coffee while she stared at the fire licking the logs in the stove.

"Evie," I said quietly, "what happened?"

She looked at me blankly for a minute and then turned back toward the stove. "I'm tired," she said dully.

I got up and took the mug from her hands. Putting a pillow at the end of the couch, I helped her lie down and covered her with the thickest quilt I could find in the cedar chest. I sat back down in the chair and watched Evie as her eyelids finally grew heavy and she slept. The sounds I heard were magnified in the quiet house: the ice hitting the windowpanes, logs crackling in the wood stove, and the hitching breaths of my battered best friend. My eyes spilled over with tears and I finally fell into a fitful sleep.

The next morning, I woke up to see Evie sitting up on the edge of the couch staring out the window. The sleet had stopped sometime in the early morning hours and the sun was shining heartily, making the day almost pleasant for mid-November in northern Missouri.

"Why are you my friend?" she asked quietly.

"What?" I sat up and brushed my tangled hair out of my eyes.

"Why are you my friend? Why do you put up with all this? And, don't give me any of that 'because you're funny and make me laugh' crap."

I thought for a moment, choosing my words carefully. "You *are* funny and you *do* make me laugh."

"Great." She threw the blanket aside and started to get up.

"Stop, I wasn't finished. Evie, you get me, you know? You let me talk about my mom and don't get weird about it. You make me laugh every day. You help me be brave when I'm around you."

"Yeah, or at least not such a giant chicken anyway."

"See? You're my best friend." I held up my hands helplessly.

"Okay, St. Louis. You don't have to get all mushy on me." She attempted a smile but winced and wiped her mouth with the back of her hand. When she brought her hand away, a streak of blood covered it. She turned the right side of her face to me and I gasped. Her lip was swollen to twice its normal size and she had a blue and black bruise growing on her cheek. I went to the kitchen on shaky legs to get some ice.

"Evie, can you please tell me what happened last night?" I asked, coming back into the living room and handing her the ice pack. "Did your mom do that to you?"

Evie paused, seeming to replay something in her mind. She took a deep breath. Her voice sounded robotic when she started talking. "Mom got home from work and I was already in bed asleep so she started drinking. When she ran out of liquor, she woke me up and made me drive her into town to buy more. On our way back, we got a couple of miles from home and she asked me to take her over to Tony's house."

"Who's Tony?"

"Tony beat her up last month and stole her money. Great guy. So, I told her no." Evie winced as she moved the ice pack to her cheek. "All of a sudden, she hit me in the side of the head with her bottle. I swerved and the car slid off the road and she kept hitting me, so I climbed out to get away from her. She screamed at me that I was no daughter to her anymore and drove off. She left me on the side of the road in my pajamas, you know? Like, whose mom does that? I'm going to have to revoke her nomination for Mother of the Year." She attempted another weak smile, wincing again and wiping away a fresh spot of blood.

"It's okay," I said. "Will you please let us help you now?"

Evie sat quietly for a moment looking at me. "Yeah, St. Louis, I'll let you help me now."

A few hours later, my dad finally got home, calling out as he walked in the back door. "Marissa? Your car's here. Are you sick?" His voice trailed off when he saw Evie and me sitting in the living room. Despite the ice, Evie's lip was still swollen and the bruise on her cheek now threatened to overtake her right eye.

"Dammit," Dad said, setting down his file box and bag. He strode into the living room and sat down gently on the other side of Evie on the couch. "Genevieve, who did this to you?"

Evie looked at me.

"It's okay," I whispered.

"My mom," Evie choked out, looking down at the floor. A tear ran down the length of her nose and splashed onto the blanket.

"Genevieve, has she done this before?"

"Not this bad. She usually doesn't hit my face." Evie drew in a shaky breath and leaned against me.

"Okay." My dad sat for a moment, pulling out a butterscotch and rolling the candy between his fingers. "Okay," he said again. "Girls, go upstairs and get dressed. Marissa, get the bags and boxes from the storage room and put them in the truck. Genevieve, dear, what time does your mom leave for work?"

"She usually leaves about two o'clock."

Dad stood up and went into his office, closing the windowed French doors behind him. I watched him jab the numbers on his phone and begin pacing. After a few seconds, he started talking to whoever picked up the line. I ushered Evie upstairs to get dressed and wash up a bit. While she was changing, I went to the room next to mine and pulled out four of our largest suitcases and two boxes with handles. Dad came up the stairs and helped me carry them out to the truck. Then, we went back inside and walked Evie out.

A few minutes later, we were parked in Evie's driveway, staring at the trailer. Dad held out his hand to her. "The key, please."

She dropped her key ring with the purple rabbit's foot keychain into my dad's palm.

"Wait here," Dad said, getting out of the truck. We watched as he climbed the concrete blocks and pounded on the back door. When no one answered, he unlocked the door and disappeared inside. A few minutes later, he came back out to the truck. "She's gone. Marissa, help me get the suitcases?"

The trailer was filled with the stench of stale cigarette smoke. Too much furniture was shoved into the small living area and bags of bottles covered the kitchenette floor. Evie looked mortified and I reached out my hand to her.

"It's okay," I said, squeezing her hand.

"Genevieve, where's your room, dear?"

Evie led us down a narrow hallway to a room in the back corner of the trailer. Evie stood in the middle of her room, looking lost. Dad took her arm and looked right into her eyes. Speaking gently, he asked her to show us what she wanted to take with her. She came out of her stupor a bit and started showing me what she wanted packed. For the next half hour, there was a flurry of activity in the little trailer. Evie and I filled suitcases with clothes, shoes, CDs, and books. Then, Dad packed them into the truck. Finally, the room had been stripped almost bare and I asked Evie if she was ready to go.

"Just a second," she said, disappearing into her mom's room. She came out clutching a photo of an eight-year-old Evie and a younger version of her mother smiling at the camera. She looked around once more and then went right out and climbed into the truck. Dad locked the door and pulled it closed behind him, closing a business card in the screen door.

"What was that?" I asked as he came down the steps.

"The number of a lawyer friend of mine who will be contacting her about a transfer of guardianship." He looked down at me and put his arm around my shoulders. "You did a good thing, Peanut," he said, guiding me toward the truck. "Let's go home."

CHAPTER 10

Friday evening, Evie sat on the edge of my bed making comments about each outfit I tried on: "Too much skin. It's a first date. Not enough skin, he'll think you're a prude."

Finally, we settled on a pair of jeans, boots, and a sweater for my first date. At eight o'clock, Evie was finishing curling my hair when the doorbell rang. I peeked out the window and saw a blue vintage Mustang parked below. Dad's voice rumbled from the living room as I swept my fingers through my long hair and checked it out in the mirror.

I shook my head. "It looks great, but I'll end up pulling it up in a bun before the night's over."

"At least give him a chance to run his fingers through it!" Evie snorted. The bruise on her cheek had settled and the swelling in her lip had all but disappeared.

"Shut it." I grabbed my coat from the back of my desk chair. My hand on the door, I turned back. "Are you sure you don't want me to reschedule? Stay home with you tonight?"

"You need to get your head checked, St. Louis," was her reply. She pushed me out the door and I headed down the steps, running my tongue over my teeth. I'd forgotten to check and make sure there was no lipstick on them. I glanced in the mirror on the landing. *Good to go.*

I took a deep breath and rounded the corner. "Hey."

"Wow," Grant breathed, "you look great!"

My dad cleared his throat. "Have her back by eleven in one piece."

"Yes, sir. Are you ready?"

I nodded and took my purse from the coatrack near the front door.

I followed Grant to his car while trying to get my nerves under control. I wondered how many people had actually barfed on their first dates and decided

I was going to have to look it up when I got home. Grant opened the car door for me and I climbed in, trying to look graceful and sure of myself, but knowing I was probably failing miserably. The car upholstery smelled like his cologne and I resisted the urge to turn around backwards in my seat and bury my nose in it.

"So, what do you think of Culvers Grove so far?" He glanced over at me as he started the engine.

"It's okay. I've met a lot of nice people here."

"Aren't you bored? You've got to miss some things about St. Louis."

I sat there in the passenger seat as the car tore through the darkness of the country thinking of about a million things I missed. Like, my mom, my friends, my house, and the bagels at the diner on the corner. "Yeah," I said, "there are things I miss. But, I'm planning to go to SLU, so I guess I'll be there again after I graduate."

"I'm going to community college right now, but I want to go to the University of Missouri in Kansas City to study finance as soon as my dad can spare me around the shop." Grant turned to me and raised an eyebrow. "What are you going to study?"

"Medicine. I want to be an oncologist."

"That has to do with..."

"Cancer. I want to help people like my mom."

"Oh, yeah."

The drive was quiet for a few moments then. I barely breathed, worried that Grant was yet another person who was uncomfortable talking about my mother's death.

"I'm sorry about that," Grant said. "It must have been rough. I can't imagine what it would feel like."

I exhaled the breath I had been holding and stared into the darkness. "It's getting better," I said. "Where are we going tonight?"

"I thought we could go to dinner at the café in Eagleton and then, I don't know, maybe we could go see a movie?"

"That sounds fine," I said.

Dinner was pretty uneventful, meaning, I didn't spill an entire glass of water in my lap or accidentally throw a meatball at Grant's nose. In fact, it was a very nice dinner and he offered to pay at the end, even though I had my wallet out and ready. I insisted on paying for our tickets to the movie and we shared a tub of popcorn. During one of the fight scenes, Grant reached over and took my hand in his. My heart did a little flutter and I took a deep breath. His hand felt warm and rough from hard work. I scooted down in my seat and leaned a little toward him, needing a drink, but not wanting my hand back. I was pretty sure at that point, I would have died of dehydration rather than let go of his hand. When the lights came up at the end of the movie, we stood up and walked out, still holding hands.

"Can I take you out again sometime soon?" he asked later as we stood on the front porch of my house.

I could make out the figures of my dad and Evie crouched by the window spying on us. "Yeah, I think that can be arranged." I smiled.

Then it happened.

Grant looked down into my eyes and leaned in close. The smell of his cologne was all around me and he tilted my chin up with a fingertip. I closed my eyes and felt his lips brush my own. I breathed in deeply and smiled as he pulled away, the feel of his lips still lingering on mine.

"Goodnight, Marissa," he said in a raspy voice. He cleared his throat, "and I'll see you next weekend, Mr. Anderson!"

I saw the figures at the window dip out of sight. With a smile, a toss of his hair and a wink, Grant got in his car and pulled out.

I sighed and opened the front door.

"Oh, Grant's so dreamy!" My dad made a kissy noise.

"I *love* you, Grant!" Evie swooned.

"Stuff it," I growled, walking past them into the kitchen. I pulled a can of soda out of the refrigerator and cracked it open.

Dad and Evie followed me in, sniggering.

"So, tell me all about it," said Evie.

"Yes, do tell," Dad said.

I grabbed Evie's arm and pulled her up the stairs with a glare at my dad.

"Aw, come on!" he called. "I don't want to miss out on the girl talk!"

"Goodnight, Dad!"

We clambered up the stairs and went into my room.

"So?" Evie bounced down on the futon, its springs squeaking in protest.

"It was nice."

"Nice? You went on a date with Grant Hoffman! Do you know how many girls would have loved to trade places with you tonight?"

I smiled and did a twirl in the middle of the room. "Fine, it was amazing. Seriously, it couldn't have been a better first date. He took me to dinner at that café in Eagleton and then we went to see a movie."

"Are you going out with him again?" she asked.

I sat down on the edge of my bed and took a drink of soda. "Yeah, I'm pretty sure. I don't know.

I guess he'll call me if he wants to go out again. No biggie, either way," I said, trying to play it cool.

Evie stared at me, mouth open. "You are so frustrating, St. Louis!"

I lay back on my bed, looking up at the ceiling. I wouldn't ever admit it to Evie, but going on my very first date had been perfect.

A few days later, Dad came out of his office rubbing his eyes.

"You okay?" I looked up from my book.

"Yeah, where's Genevieve?" he asked.

"I don't know. I think she's upstairs in my room listening to music. Do you want me to get her?"

"No, no," Dad groaned as he sat down on the couch next to me. "I heard from Nick this morning. Genevieve's mom signed away her rights as a guardian. He went over to her trailer and the petition was taped to the door."

"What does that mean?"

"Well," Dad pulled a butterscotch from the bowl on the coffee table. "I guess it means that Evie will have to stay with us for little while longer."

I cleared my throat. "Do you think we could help her find her dad?"

He looked down at his hands. "I have a private detective friend that owes me a favor. Why don't you get me all of the information you can and I'll see what I can do when I drive down there later this week."

"Okay."

Dad got up and headed to the kitchen for more coffee. He stopped in the archway behind the couch. "And, Marissa?"

"Yeah?"

"Let's not tell Genevieve about her mom. I'm afraid it would break her heart to know that her mom gave her up so easily."

Later that week, Dad was on his way to St. Louis, in part to turn in some paperwork to his bosses, and in part to talk to his detective friend. I had managed to gather a little bit of information about Evie's dad, but she was very shaky on the details. She told me that his name was Jeff Warren and he was ex-military. She wasn't sure which branch. Her mom had met him at a bar. He had lived with her mom for about two years, and then, when Evie was almost one, he had disappeared.

"He sent this when I turned ten." She pulled out a faded card with a rose on it from her suitcase.

I took it and turned it over in my hands. "To my beautiful rose," I read aloud. I opened the card.

"May your birthday bring you all the joy you have brought me," Evie said along with me. "Look here," she said, turning over the envelope, "it's postmarked Austin. He could be an oil tycoon or a ranch owner." Her eyes lit up as she tucked the card away again in the suitcase. "He could be anything, St. Louis! And, as soon as I graduate, I'm going to Austin to try to find him!"

There were so many things wrong with this statement that I felt sick, but I didn't want to hurt Evie's feelings. I had read once that only twelve percent of father-daughter reunions of this nature were gauged positively by both parties. Who was to say her dad would be any better than her mom? Or even if he wanted to know her? I took one look at Evie's hopeful face, though, and knew I couldn't say any of those things.

I changed the subject instead. "I hope you don't mind sharing your space with all of these boxes right now. Dad said that as soon as he and Grant get the shed ready, we can start storing the boxes in there and get this cleaned out for you."

"I can't believe your dad's being so cool about this." She hung her clothes in the closet. "It's really nice of you both." She smiled, but a sadness crept into her eyes.

"No worries." I made up her bed with a comforter fresh out of the laundry.

A horn honked outside and Evie and I both looked at each other for a moment.

"Are you expecting anyone?" I asked.

"No, you?"

"Huh uh, let's go see who it is."

Running to my room, we peered out the front windows to the driveway below. Grant stepped out of his car. He looked up to my window and waved. I felt a hot flush rise up to my ears.

"Oh, man, he is one smitten kitten," Evie mumbled, rolling her eyes.

I ran downstairs and let Grant in the door.

He gave me a peck on the cheek and handed me a bouquet of flowers. "Sorry, they wilted a little in my car." He fidgeted back and forth from one foot to the other.

Did he know how handsome he looked in those faded blue jeans and that crisp white shirt? "What are you doing here?" I took the flowers from him and put them in a vase, thankful to have something to do with my hands.

"I came by to see if you would do me a big favor."

"That depends," I eyed him suspiciously. "What's the favor?"

"Well, my cousin's getting married at the beginning of December, and well, my dad's making me go. We can bring a date, and..." Grant trailed off, looking up at me desperately to save him.

"...and you want me to go with you?" I finished for him.

"Would you? I know weddings can be boring, especially when you don't know anyone, but we had so much fun last weekend I thought, maybe, I don't know...you'd make it fun." He looked at me and flashed a smile.

I turned away from him. "That's a long time away. You sure you're not going to find someone else you'd rather take?"

"I don't want anyone else," he said, his voice close to my ear.

I turned around. "Why haven't you called or texted? An email? A smoke signal?"

He laughed, his cheeks blushing bright crimson. "I know I haven't called, but I've been busy with work and school." He looked at me. "I'm not sure what to do here, Marissa." He rubbed the back of his neck. "I didn't want to scare you away."

My mind reeled with the ridiculousness of that statement. "You're not scaring me," I said, taking a step closer.

"I understand if you can't go."

I smiled. "I'll go. But, this doesn't count as a date so you'll owe me one of those, too."

"Thanks," he said. "I'll have the prettiest girl at the wedding with me."

Now it was my turn to blush.

"You know," Grant said, moving closer, "you really are beautiful." He reached up, pushed a tendril of hair away from my face, and smiled. I leaned in and closed my eyes and he met me halfway, wrapping his arms around me and kissing me with his soft lips. I drew in a sharp breath, the feeling leaving my legs.

He pulled away and looked down at me. "Wow."

"Yeah," I crooned, "wow."

"Two weeks from tomorrow," he said, his hand on the doorknob. "Bye."

I waved and watched as he jogged down the porch steps and walked across the yard to his car. He waved as he started his car and backed out the driveway.

"I feel like I should be making fun of you for something," Evie squinted at me as she came down the stairs.

"How much did you see?"

"I didn't see anything, but you're bright red." Evie smiled and elbowed me in the ribs.

CHAPTER 11

Evie sat on the bed for a minute, flipping through the channels on the television before finally turning it off and walking over to the window. We had all been pretty quiet since dinner. Dad had spent the last hour working in his office, emerging once in a while to fill his coffee cup.

This first Thanksgiving without my mom had been hard.

"You want to go for a walk?" Evie asked, her breath making a circle of fog on the pane of glass.

"Right now? It's like the Antarctic out there."

"I know. I need to get out of the house, though."

I suddenly realized that Evie was spending Thanksgiving without her mom, too. "I guess we could go for a short walk up to the road and back again. Give me a minute to get dressed." Evie went to her room while I pulled on a pair of sweats and a pair of jeans over those. I shoved my feet into two pairs of socks and yanked on a sweatshirt over my pajama shirt. We met in the kitchen, shrugging on coats, hats, and gloves.

Dad walked in to refill his coffee cup again. "Where are you two off to?" He looked outside and shivered.

"We're going to go for a quick walk." I wrapped a long scarf around and around my neck.

"Okay, but be careful and only go a little way. It's too cold to be out long."

"We'll be back soon, Mr. A." Evie opened the back door.

I steeled myself against the cold and followed her out into the night. We grabbed two flashlights from the shelf near the door and I started walking toward the driveway.

"No, St. Louis, this way. I want to show you something."

I followed Evie around the back of the barn and we began walking into the woods. The night around us was so quiet I could hear nothing but the crunching of the snow under our boots. The moonlight spilled through the leafless trees, creating a skeleton of shadows on the floor of the forest. We stopped for a moment while Evie swung her flashlight around.

I turned and panicked for a moment when I couldn't see the house.

She followed my gaze. "It's behind the barn. We can always follow our footprints back."

"Great, just like Hansel and Gretel," I mumbled, straining my eyes against the dark. "And how did that story go?"

She walked along a path covered with deer tracks and small animal footprints.

I could hear rushing water way up in the distance. "Where are we going?" I pulled my coat tightly around me, trying to block out the wind.

"Keep up," she called back over her shoulder. We climbed down a snow-covered embankment, the sound getting closer.

Up ahead, I could make out the glint of water in the moonlight. "We're going to die out here, aren't we?"

"No," Evie said a second before both she and her light disappeared from view.

"Evie!" My voice shook.

"Down here, St. Louis!"

I climbed down into a gulley and found her hunched inside the mouth of a cave. I shook my head. "Right. Trip's over. Let's go back, okay?" My flashlight beam shook in the air. "I don't really want to tangle with a bear tonight."

"Oh, come on, you big chicken! I've been in here a million times. Come look!"

Against my better judgement, I followed her down into the cave. It was a tight fit, but as soon as we made it around the first bend, the cave spread out in all directions around us. We were in a huge cavern, the sound of water dripping echoing around us. My breath hung in the air as I flashed my light around. The walls were shiny with dampness and there was a small pool of water on the floor near the back.

"What do you think?" Evie sat down on a rock. "I found this place before you all moved in. It stays really cool in the summer. Look." She shined her flashlight against the wall to her left. "See those things scratched into the wall? You think they might be Native American?"

I walked over and took a closer look. On the wall, there were what appeared to be letters of some sort. "Hold on." I pulled my phone from my pocket and took a picture, the flash lighting up the cavern.

"Do you get anything in here?" she asked from behind my shoulder.

I didn't have to ask what she meant. I shook my head. "I don't think so."

She took a candle from her backpack and placed it on the huge rock near the mouth of the cavern. When she lit it, the glow cast eerie shadows on the walls and made the etchings seem almost like they were moving.

"Creepy, creepy, creepy," I said quietly.

"Would you shut up?" Evie took her phone from her coat pocket. "I've read that you can play flute music to call the spirits." She swiped through a couple screens and the cavern was filled with the piping lilting melody.

My eyes scanned around, and the hairs on my arms raised. "Evie," I whispered, "something's happening."

"What?"

"Every time something starts to happen and I am going to see something, I get this weird feeling beforehand. And, it's happening right now."

We sat down next to one another on a rock and listened to the music playing, the melody dancing in and out of the caverns. Suddenly, a flash of red lit up the entire room. I watched as a fire materialized in the middle of the floor. I could make out figures crouched around it.

"Do you see that?" I hissed.

I closed my eyes for a minute and when I opened them, the scene in front of me had become clearer. I could now see long black hair pulled back in braids and the hairs on the fur skins they were wearing stood out clearly against the backdrop of the fire.

Dropping my flashlight, the scene in front of me vanished. I felt like something was sitting on my chest and I had just enough time to look up at Evie before I fell off the rock and landed on the ground with a thud. My eyelids felt heavy and I watched through slits as Evie blew out the candle, drowning the cave in darkness.

"Time to go, St. Louis," she said, her voice shaking. She helped me to a standing position and duck walked me out of the cave.

When we were back in the woods, I regained strength in my legs and immediately stalked off. I didn't stop until I was back in my bedroom, sitting on my bed.

"What did you see?" Evie asked me for the fiftieth time as she came into the room.

I glared at her and opened the soda she handed me.

"Come on, St. Louis, don't hold out on me! I can't see the stuff you can!"

"I'm not sure what I saw," I said after a long drink. "I think I saw a fire and some people crouched around it."

"Whoa…" Evie breathed, sitting down on the futon. "What else?"

"Nothing. I sort of thought that was enough!" I snapped.

"Easy, St. Louis."

"It creeps me out. Being able to see stuff like that isn't normal!"

"Who ever said you were normal?" Evie laughed. "Come on. It had to be kind of cool, right? Please, tell me what you saw?"

I sighed. I tried to tell her about what I saw, but my words were jumbled and I couldn't describe it well enough. I threw my hands up in frustration.

Evie sat up on the edge of the futon. She squinted at me and then got up and pulled down a pile of copy paper from my shelf. Pulling out a pencil from my cup, she held them both out to me.

I looked up at her and shook my head. "What's that for?"

"I have an idea." She nodded to the paper. "Do you think you could draw it?"

"I can't even draw a stick person; let alone what I saw tonight."

"Just try, okay? You never know until you try."

I took the paper and pencil with a sigh and closed my eyes. I touched the pencil to the paper and I started drawing. It was only after a few minutes that I realized I hadn't opened my eyes yet. I forced my eyelids to open.

Evie was standing next to me, mouth and eyes open wide, staring at the page in my lap. "Liar," she whispered.

I looked down at the paper and threw it and the pencil across the room. I stood up and started pacing.

She went over to the corner and retrieved the paper. On it was a detailed pencil drawing of the scene in the cave. Sketched to perfect proportion with shadowing and depth, it looked like a professional artist had created it.

"Wow," she said, looking up at me. "How did you do that?"

"I don't know." I looked down at my hands as if they had betrayed me. "I don't know how or why I did that! Look!" I ran to the desk and started rummaging around in the backpack hanging from the back of my desk chair. I pulled out my sketchbook from art class and opened it. It was filled with mis-shapen apples and portraits of people that looked like they had been stricken with some disfiguring disease. "Look at this and then tell me how I drew that!" I gestured emphatically at the drawing she held in her hands.

"Wow," Evie said again.

"Would you say something useful?"

"Can you draw more?"

I threw the sketchbook at her and stood fuming in the middle of my bedroom.

"St. Louis, listen. There's something really special about you. Have you ever heard of automatic writing?"

I shook my head.

"Well, there are people out there who can close their eyes, and like, channel a spirit. That spirit uses their body as a vessel of communication through writing. I watched a documentary on it one time. This lady from Omaha was an automatic writer and she showed the film crew a sample of her normal writing. Then she went into some sort of a trance and started writing with her eyes closed. When she was finished, she held up a sheet with writing that was totally not her own. The film crew showed several of her samples and none of them looked the same. Maybe you can do something like that except with drawing."

"I don't know," I said. My legs were weak and I sat down at my desk. "Why is all this stuff happening to me? Why now?"

"Maybe you've always been a creepy art kid at heart." She smiled. "Come on, try drawing something else?" She placed the paper and pencil in front of me on the desk. "Please?"

I took the pencil with a sigh and closed my eyes again. Again, the pencil started moving as if it had a mind of its own across the paper. I could hear Evie standing next to me, breathing shallowly. After several minutes, my hand felt like my own again and I stopped drawing.

Evie exhaled and took the pencil out of my hand. "Open your eyes," she said softly, putting her hand on my shoulder, "and don't freak out this time, okay?"

I blinked a couple of times and looked down. There on the paper was a drawing of a bedroom I'd never seen before. Near the window in the picture was an old man sitting in a chair. The old man's eyes were so real they looked like they could cry real tears and the wrinkles on his face were lifelike.

"Who *is* that?" Evie breathed.

"How should I know? I've never seen him before!"

"Wow." Evie leaned down to look more closely.

"There you go again. Something useful, please," I hissed.

"Okay, fine. I think you should enter that one in the art contest at school."

I pushed the paper away and got up. "I don't understand. This is all too much. Especially tonight." I shook my head. "I don't want to do this anymore tonight."

"Okay, St. Louis. We're done." Evie gathered the papers and slid them into a folder. She placed them high on the shelf in the closet. "There. No more tonight."

I nodded and sat down on my bed. "Thanks."

Evie stood uncertainly in the middle of my room. She crossed her arms in front of her chest and rubbed her hands along her upper arms. "Wanna watch a cheesy Christmas movie?"

I pressed my lips together and pushed the images from the cave and the drawings away. "Sure."

Evie flopped down on the futon and turned on the television. We found an old movie and settled down to watch.

Dad's voice floated up the stairs. "You girls don't stay up too late. We're headed out early tomorrow for Christmas shopping."

Evie groaned. She looked at me. "You do realize I'm buying your dad a shirt that's *not* flannel, right!"

"I heard that and don't bother. I won't wear it," Dad called.

I snickered. "Believe me, flannel won't seem so bad this summer when he's wearing blue jean cut offs and black socks!"

It snowed that night and by the time we rolled into town the next morning, the town of Chillicothe looked like the front of a holiday card. The winter sun kissed the blanket of white, casting everything in a sparkling pink glow. We spent the morning shopping along Main Street. I bought a really nice pen for my dad. It felt heavy in my hand and I was able to have it engraved with his name. I was sure he would love it. For Andy and Tristan, I picked up a DVD set of their favorite ghost hunting series, and for Jessica, I found a pair of headlight eyelashes for her Jeep. I also picked out a chenille scarf and gloves for Grant that perfectly matched his eyes.

Evie suggested we separate to buy gifts for each other and while she was in another shop, I went into a jewelry store and found a beautiful silver necklace.

It had a delicate chain and a rectangular charm. On the charm was printed the word *Strength*. It was perfect. I had it wrapped and headed outside with my bags, walking toward my dad's truck.

"Marissa!" Evie came bounding across the street, a car narrowly missing her. It honked and she waved.

"Be a little more careful!"

"I'm fine," she panted. "Look at this!" She swept a bag out from behind her back and pulled out a box. "I found this at the antique store! Can you believe they only wanted two dollars for it?" I took the box and wiped the dust from the cover. It read: *The Ouija or Wonderful Talking Board.* "Check it out." She opened the top.

"I don't know about this." I eyed the board warily. "I've heard a lot of bad stuff can happen from those."

Evie rolled her eyes. "I thought you'd be a little more excited." She stuffed it back in the bag. "Anyway, look what I got for your dad!" True to her word, she had bought him a long-sleeved red and blue striped shirt – one hundred percent cotton.

"Good grief. He'll look like the fourth of July!"

"At least he won't look like a lumberjack anymore!" She unlocked the door to the truck and held it open for me. We stuffed our packages on the seat and then walked across the street to the restaurant. Dad wasn't there yet, so we sat down and ordered a couple of sodas.

Evie pulled off her coat, putting it in the booth next to her. "Do you think we should try to call the spirits in the cave tonight?"

"There's absolutely no way I'm going to do any sort of calling of any spirits. Way too scary."

"Chicken," Evie muttered out of the corner of her mouth as the bell above the door rang.

Dad walked into the restaurant and the waitress pointed to our table. He walked over with a toothy grin. "Santa's going to be very good to you girls this year!"

CHAPTER 12

I managed to talk Evie out of going back to the cave that night, and the next afternoon, we were all hanging out in my room, watching television and talking. Evie sat with Tristan as she tried to teach him to hand knit. He wanted to finish a scarf for his mom for Christmas, but at the moment, he was covered in yarn and his and Evie's hands were tangled together. I flipped through the messages from Grant on my phone, trying to ignore Andy. He was sprawled out on my bed after eating half the leftovers in the refrigerator, belching occasionally and swearing off ever eating that much again, which he did at least three times every week.

Evie looked up at me and mouthed, "Can I show them your drawings?"

I considered a moment. *What would they think about this? Would they think I was weird?* Then, *would they want me to use this new trick in an investigation?* Finally, I nodded and Evie got up to pull the pages from the shelf in my closet.

"Guys, take a look at this." She placed the two drawings side by side on the bed next to Andy.

I walked over and stood by Evie.

Andy rolled over with a grunt and then let out a low whistle. "Where'd you get those mad skills, Evester? Did you take a class down at the career center, 'cause last time I checked, I had it all over you in sketch."

"Not me." Evie jutted a thumb in my direction. "Your girl here."

"You didn't tell me you could draw," Tristan's voice came from behind me. He had joined us and stood looking down at the drawings, a string of yarn following him across the floor.

I swallowed. "I can't. Draw. Really. Most of the time, they turn out looking like a trampled cat."

Andy raised an eyebrow.

"Seriously, I drew a horse for my mom when I was eight. It looked like it had mange. I haven't improved since."

"I've seen her drawings. She sucks," Evie confirmed with a nod of her head.

"Thanks," I muttered.

Andy leaned in. "So, what exactly am I looking at here?" He gestured at the scene from the cave.

"It's something I saw the other night that Evie didn't."

Tristan glanced at me. "This is what you see, you know, when you...?"

I crossed my arms over my chest. "Sometimes."

"I think she's an automatic writer." Evie bit her bottom lip.

"That's super rare." Tristan's eyes were wide.

"I know, but do you have another explanation for those?" Evie gestured at the papers.

Tristan turned to me. "What do you think?"

Suddenly, everyone else was looking at me, too.

I pressed my lips together and shook my head slowly. "I don't know." I shrugged. "I've never done anything like this before. I wouldn't have even done *this* if Evie hadn't asked me to try to draw what I saw."

"What about that one?" Tristan nodded at the picture of the old man.

I shook my head. "No idea."

We stared down at the pictures.

"Who's that?" Andy pointed a long finger at the window where the old man sat.

Tristan, Evie, and I leaned forward over the pictures.

"Oh, I see her now," Tristan breathed.

There, in the window, was the faint outline of a figure. She held out her arms toward the old man.

"I have no idea," I said. "He looks like he's so sad."

"Hold on!" Andy grabbed his backpack from the floor and pulled a rumpled piece of newspaper out of the front pocket. He laid it on the bed next to the pictures. "It's an ad for the auction of the old Dietrich place."

"And you're carrying it around in your backpack because why?" Evie cocked her head to the side.

He stopped and feigned disbelief. "The auction circuit is what all the cool kids are doing these days. I thought you knew."

Evie pursed her lips and threw her middle finger up at him.

"I think this might be the man from Marissa's drawing. So, I saw this article last week and I thought it might be a good place for us to investigate. I mean, the cemetery's good and all, but I thought we could go somewhere with a," Andy paused, searching for the words, "fresher soul?"

Tristan closed his eyes and shook his head. "Honestly, Andy. Tact. Try it sometime." He plopped back down on the futon and untangled the yarn from his hand, tossing it at the floor. "That's it. She's getting a gift card from Barnes and Noble again this year."

"No, listen," Andy plunged on, "I asked my dad about it and he said that Old August Dietrich lived there all his life and when his wife died, he went crazy."

"We all go a little crazy when we lose someone," Tristan said.

"No, like, really crazy." Andy used a finger to circle the air around his ear. "Really off the charts. My dad said he started keeping to himself, making these weird sculptures and hanging them up all around his farm." Andy handed the pictures and ad to Evie before sitting on the bed again. "Anyway, he died at the beginning of the year and the bank is auctioning it off next weekend. I drove out there a couple weeks ago and it was completely abandoned. What do you think?" He looked up at us expectantly.

"What do *you* think?" Evie asked me.

I sat down on the futon and drew my knees up to my chest. "Well," I said carefully, "if you're sure it's abandoned and we won't get in trouble for being out there, I guess I'm game." Once the words were out of my mouth, my stomach started spinning.

"Me, too," said Evie.

"And me, three," said Tristan.

"Tomorrow's Sunday. Let's head out from here around, what do you say, six?"

"Dad's not going to like me going out on a school night. We'll have to be back by eleven."

"Totally doable," Evie said. "Oh, I forgot to show you guys what I got at the antique store yesterday!" She jumped up from the chair and darted into her room. A minute later, she returned, carrying the Ouija board. She put it in the middle of the floor and sat down.

"Oh, cool!" Andy rolled off the bed and onto the floor next to Evie. "Does it have the planchette?"

"It's an original." Tristan sat down next to Andy. He looked at the cover of the box reverently. "The Kennard Novelty Company started making these in the 1890s. Great find, Patton."

"Thanks!"

My heart raced as I looked at the board. Something about the air in the room changed with its arrival. It almost vibrated. "Come on, guys," I heard myself close to whining. "Can we please put that thing away?"

"We can, if it makes you uncomfortable." Tristan's eyes were unwavering.

"Yeah, St. Louis, but, you know, it could be really cool!"

I looked at their eager faces, sighed, and joined my friends on the floor. "Fine, but if this goes weird, I'm out."

"Do you know how to work it?" Tristan whispered to Evie. He rolled up the sleeves of his sweater and leaned in.

"I've been reading these." Evie held up the instruction manual and a weathered old paperback.

"*Calling the Spirits*," Andy read, grabbing the paperback. He started flipping through the pages.

"So, what do we do?" I swallowed hard, trying to ignore the vibration that had now spread into the floor and walls.

"Well, we all sit around it..."

"Check."

"...and put our fingertips on the planchette. Then, we ask it things. It's supposed to start moving on its own and answering our questions." Evie shrugged a shoulder.

"Cool," Tristan breathed.

"Yeah, cool," I said, already worried that whatever was going to happen when we started would hit *me* harder than anyone else. *It's hard to be brave when everything seems to happen to me.* I put my fingertips on the planchette.

Immediately, it started to move. At first, slowly moving in a circle, in seconds, it began to spin around the board faster and faster.

"Is there someone here with us?" Evie asked.

The planchette stopped whirling and edged up toward the word, yes.

I swallowed as the lampshade on my desk quivered.

"Who are you?" Evie asked clearly. The planchette hesitated for a moment and then swung in an arc to the letter S. It swung back to the letter A and then ended on the letter M before starting its circular march again.

"Sam," I breathed, looking up at Andy for a moment.

He nodded and looked back down. "We're all here."

"Is your name Sam?" Evie asked. The planchette swung to yes. "Okay, what should I ask it now?" she hissed.

"I don't know, ask him how old he is," Andy suggested.

"Sam, how old were you when you died?"

The lampshade shook and a cool breeze wrapped its way around me. I closed my eyes and tried to block it out. When I opened them, I watched the planchette go from one to nine.

"Nineteen. How did you die?" Evie asked, her words coming more quickly now. The planchette began to shake and then moved to M, R, D, E, R.

"Do you think he means murder?" Tristan asked.

"It figures," Andy snorted, "we'd get a ghost who can't spell!"

Tristan elbowed him and gave him a stern look. "Don't be mean."

Andy's face fell. "I'm sorry. Sorry, Sam."

The planchette began spinning again.

"Okay, guys," I said, "Who's moving it?"

Suddenly, the planchette jerked to the left, knocking off all of the other hands. Mine alone remained on the piece of plastic. The planchette started spinning in circles while I was holding it, faster and faster. I tried to pull my hands away, but I felt like they were tied to the board.

"What the heck?" Andy reached out to place his fingertips back on the planchette. As soon as he touched it, it stopped moving. "Weird."

"Yep, weird, strange, creepy. Done." I stood up, shaking my hands. They were numb. "Evie, take that thing back to your room and put it away, please."

She nodded and put it back in the box. When she came back from returning it to her room, we all sat in uncomfortable silence, no one quite knowing what to say.

A few moments later, Andy came to the rescue. "You got any stuffing left? I'm starving!"

"Hey, guys," I said as I scooted across Andy's truck bench seat the next night.

"Hey." Tristan looked nervous and I shot a meaningful look at Evie.

The truck was silent as we bumped along down the highway.

Tristan turned to look at me. "How are things going with Grant?"

I hated that I blushed even at the mention of his name. I was glad no one could see it in the dark truck.

"They're..." Evie started.

"You. Quiet. Now." I glared at her. "They're fine. He asked me to go with him to his cousin's wedding in a couple of weeks."

"Sounds serious," Tristan said.

"Not really."

"Well, I know he's been on a lot of *first* dates," Tristan said, stressing the word first. "But, he doesn't really latch on to anyone and ask them to go out again. You must be something special, Marissa."

I swallowed, my cheeks burning. *Did Andy have the heat turned up all the way?* I cleared my throat and changed the subject. "Are you sure we're not going to get in trouble going into this house?"

"Nah." Andy kept his eyes on the road. "Like I said, I came out the other night and the way the house is set back on the road, you can't really see it from any of the neighbors' houses. We'll have to park and walk a bit, but we should be fine."

"Isn't it locked?"

Andy glanced over at me. "I forget how city you can be sometimes."

I chose to ignore the comment.

"*If* someone locks their door out here in the middle of nowhere, there's always a key hidden somewhere," Tristan explained.

Andy nodded. "Fake rock in the flowerbed."

"Fine. Do we know anything else about this place?" I asked.

"Tristan did some research last night after we left your house."

Tristan pulled out his phone on cue and began reading notes. The screen lit up his face in a blue light. "I found out that everything Andy's dad said was true. Old Man Dietrich is actually Theodore Davis Dietrich and his family built the place in the late eighteen hundreds after moving here from Germany. He met his wife, Greta, when she and her family moved to the area from Wisconsin, and when he was eighteen and she was seventeen, they got married. They never had any children, and outlived all of their other family members. While she was alive, they were a perfectly happy couple, though they kept to themselves. People said that the only time they left the farm was to go to church. They had this amazing garden of local wildflowers and their farm was featured in an issue of *The Missouri Conservationist* a few years ago, but when Greta got sick, the garden grew over with weeds. When she died, Theodore was left without anyone and he gradually started losing it.

"Those last few years he was alive, he threatened to shoot anyone that came near, including the postman and the meter reader. I found an article about the police being called out to the farm because Theodore was holding the UPS van hostage. Apparently, the driver was new and came onto the property to deliver a package. When he tried to leave, Old Man

Dietrich was sitting in the van, a shotgun across his lap, tears running down his cheeks. It took them three hours to talk him into coming out of the van. The county decided they would have to step in after the incident, but it took a while to get all the paperwork in order. When they went to pick him up, they walked in and heard music blaring. They found his decaying body in one of the upstairs bedrooms." He paused and looked down, twisting a string hanging from the edge of his sweater. "He had shot himself."

The truck was gravely quiet for a few minutes.

"He killed himself," I whispered, "in the house." The night seemed to deepen outside the truck windows.

"Then, his soul is trapped there," Evie breathed.

"People say that if you're near the house after dark, you can hear music playing," Tristan said. "Truly," he shuddered, "I don't know *who* would buy that house at the auction."

"Aw," Andy smiled, "you ruined the surprise. I was going to bid on it. It was going to be our dream home."

"Jerk," Tristan muttered, but a smile twisted the corners of his lips.

My stomach and brain argued for the rest of the drive, my brain finally winning out for the moment as Andy parked his truck in a grove of trees near the road. *Everything will be fine. There is nothing to be scared of, right?*

We sat quietly for a moment, staring out the windshield at the imposing house standing silent in the misty night. My stomach turned and my brain beat a quick retreat. *Let's just go home and watch Gilmore Girls reruns.*

"We're here," Evie said as she grabbed her backpack and climbed down out of the truck. "Might as well get started."

"Yep." Andy climbed out next and Tristan and I piled out behind him.

I stood outside the truck, gazing up at the stoic two-story house across the field. Its grey slats were broken and the paint curled up from the porch. The entire side of the house was covered in moss. My hands twisted together as the wind kicked up and tossed the tree limbs above us.

"Chickening out on me, there?" Evie hissed in my ear with a smile.

"N-no, only thinking that it looks like a ridiculously good place to find some ghosts tonight." I took a deep breath. "This is so stupid I don't even have a statistic for this one," I mumbled.

Evie elbowed me in the ribs. "Come on."

Andy put his hood up and grunted under the weight of his bag as he threw it over his shoulder.

He trudged across the field, using his free hand to yank up the waistband of his jeans along the way. The three of us followed and crouched along the hedge line, looking for signs of movement.

"I don't see anything," Tristan whispered.

Andy stood up and motioned for us to follow. Our feet left trails through the frost clinging to the tangle of long dead wildflowers as we walked. The entire area was grown over with sticker bushes and vines. Several times, a vine jumped up to grab one of us around the ankle. After the twelfth time I almost fell on my face, I grabbed Evie's arm and we struggled through the underbrush together.

A noise in the house made us all stop dead in our tracks.

"What was that?" Tristan hissed as we crouched down under the low branches of a twisted tree.

"I don't know." Evie sat up and strained her neck to see over the porch railing. "It sounded like a door slamming. Wait here."

The fear wound its way up and down my arms and legs, but I forced myself to take a deep breath. I watched tensely as Evie crept up the broken front porch steps. She army-crawled to the window and peeked in through one of the cloudy windowpanes.

"What do you see?" Andy whisper-yelled to her.

She held up a hand to us and continued to peer through the window. Suddenly, another bang rang out from the house and we all jumped. Evie started laughing.

"What's so funny, Patton?" Andy growled, dusting off the back of his pants as he stood.

"It's the back screen door opening and shutting with the wind. Here, listen, it's gonna shut again."

Sure enough, another bang and then silence.

We climbed the stairs to the front porch, Andy stopping to grab the key from under a fake rock in the flowerbed. "Let's head back there so we can get in the house before someone drives by." He motioned for us to follow him around the wraparound porch. A swing hung by one chain rocking lazily in the breeze, creaking as it went back and forth.

Tristan turned on his flashlight and shined the beam into the side yard as we walked past. "Look at that," Tristan breathed. "What *is* it?"

"I think it's a wind chime. Um, made out of doll parts," I said, as if identifying it made it any less disturbing. I shuddered as the wind chime spun and a doll head with no eyes turned toward me. The empty eye sockets seemed to follow me as I walked around to the back porch. Evie held the screen door open while Andy put the key in the lock. It turned and he pushed the weathered door open with a colossal squeak.

We stood on the threshold, none of us wanting to be the first to cross into the house.

Finally, Evie looked at us and gave a sigh of exasperation. "Honestly," she drew herself up straight and stepped into the kitchen. "See? Nothing to worry about."

"Evie!" I shouted, grabbing her by the shoulder and yanking her back.

"What the heck, St. Louis?"

"You guys saw that, right?" I backpedaled down the porch steps into the backyard.

"No, what?" they said in unison.

"Someone crossed through the doorway in front of her! Let's go!" I pleaded. "What if someone's here?"

"Okay, St. Louis," said Evie, "we'll go, but let's find out if anyone's really here before we scrap this. I mean, we drove all the way out here. And," she added with emphasis, "no one else saw anything and we were all looking at that exact same spot."

"You can go down to the truck and wait for us with the doors locked if you want." Andy dangled the keys out for me.

I shook my head, the prospect of sitting all alone in the dark wasn't any better than staying here. At least I wouldn't be alone if I stayed. "I'll stay," I said, "but you guys have to believe me. I saw some-one!"

"We believe you, Marissa; *we* just didn't see an-ything." Tristan took my hand in his. "I think it's okay. Will you come in with us?"

I nodded and reluctantly followed Andy, Tristan and Evie into the house. A fine layer of silt covered most of the surfaces in the kitchen. A vase of dusty flowers sat in the middle of the small table and a newspaper lay next to it. I felt goosebumps rise along my arms as I thought about the last moments of Theodore Dietrich's life. *Had he sat right there drinking his coffee the morning he died?* I shuddered and wrapped my arms around my chest.

"Stay here," Andy said. "We'll check it out."

He and Evie shined their flashlights into every corner of the main floor. Tristan locked the back door behind us and then walked up to check the front door. When they were done clearing the first floor, Tristan and I stayed put in the living room while Andy and Evie investigated upstairs.

"All clear!" came the shout a few minutes later from above us. Andy came down the stairs smiling. "This place is so cool! Marissa, you have to come upstairs and see what Old Man Dietrich did with the guest room."

"Be respectful!" Tristan called after him. He turned to me. "You okay going up there?"

I nodded.

"I'll be behind you the whole time."

My stomach churning uncomfortably, I climbed the stairs, watching as my hand wiped the banister free of dust. The temperature dropped as I cleared the landing and I stopped short.

Tristan drew in a breath. "You okay?" he asked.

"Yeah, why?"

"You tensed up. I thought you saw something."

"No, I didn't see anything. I suddenly got this weird feeling, though." I continued climbing the stairs and found myself facing a narrow hallway. Andy and Evie's voices came from the room to my right, but I felt drawn to the last room on the left. I fixated on that door and walked toward it.

"Hey, St. Louis, look at..." Evie trailed off as I passed her.

"Does anyone else hear that?" My eyes never wavered from the door.

"Hear what? What is she talking about?"

Tristan shrugged.

Evie followed me. "You okay?" She touched my arm.

I looked at her. Her face seemed so far away. "The music." I reached out to touch the doorknob. "Don't you hear the music?"

"Okay, St. Louis," Evie said, "cut the act. You're really weirding me out here. I'm sorry we didn't believe you earlier."

"Shhh." I put my finger to my lips and pushed open the door. My eyes registered the scene before me and I closed them. "Oh my God, Evie."

"It's the room you drew," she breathed next to me. "Well, minus the sad old guy."

I opened my eyes. "No," I said, "he's here, too."

Evie took a step back and leaned out the door. "Andy! Get down here and film," she called.

I held my breath and walked into the room. Immediately, I was struck by a powerful urge to cry. My eyes stung with hot tears and I could feel my skin begin to crawl. This room was filled with a sadness I could almost taste. I shut my eyes and tried to take a deep breath. I could hear Evie talking to Andy, but it seemed like she was a million miles away and talking through a layer of cotton. The music swept me up with it as it billowed around, the brass band playing a tune that was sad, sweet, and familiar.

"You don't see him?" I asked, my voice thick with tears.

"No, what do you see?" Evie came closer.

"I see *him.*" Tears escaped and ran down my cheeks in torrents. "He's crying. He's so sad. H-he wants to know why she left him."

Evie reached up to wipe a tear from my face with her sleeve. "Who, St. Louis? Who's sad?"

My voice came out in a whisper. "He doesn't look like he's eaten for days. He keeps calling out 'Greta!'" I made my way over to the window, one trembling step in front of the other.

He sat facing the window, his back ramrod straight and his white hair patchy and tangled above his ears. I saw the moonlight glint off the shotgun in his lap. The smell that rose from him coated my tongue with despair and loneliness. *I understand. I do.* I found myself reaching out to touch the man's shoulder.

As my hand brushed his shoulder, he dropped his head. "She left me. I'm so alone. My Greta. My Greta." His voice was barely a whisper.

I understand. I've felt that way, too.

He turned eyes cloudy with cataracts up to me. They registered for a moment and then a snarl wound its way up from his core, shaking my hand as it rested on his shoulder. He opened his mouth and a screeching sound emanated from him, animalistic and raw. "Get out!" he screamed, eyes bugging and spit flying from his mouth. "Get out of my house! Leave me alone! Get out!"

I recoiled and stumbled back, tripping over my feet and falling. I crashed to the floor, my hands flying up to cover my ears. The music amped up a notch, punctuated by his screams, pelting my eardrums to the point I thought they would burst. Looking up at the window, I saw the form floating just outside, ethereal and full of love.

It was his Greta.

He can't get to her.

It was the last thought I had before darkness pressed in from all sides, blocking out the noise. Pressure built and I closed my eyes, seeking solace from the scene in front of me.

When I opened my eyes, I saw Theodore and Greta, or rather, younger versions of themselves. He wore coveralls and a red plaid shirt and his hair was jet black and slicked back on his head. Greta wore a calico dress, her hair twisted into a loose bun, her cheeks red with color as Theodore swung her around the room, his feet beating rhythm to the music swelling around them. A record player in the corner of the room played *Chattanooga Choo Choo,* a song I'd heard my grandmother play a million times. Theodore spun Greta and then dipped her, leaning over her to kiss her rosebud lips. His eyes sparkled and her laughter filled the room.

They loved each other. So much.

I heard voices and felt hands under my back. My friends carried me from the room, the scene fading, leaving the man by himself in front of the window again. Alone. Tears running down his face. The moment we crossed into the hallway, the door slammed behind us.

I shook off the pressure and fought to regain my feet. "Let me down!" As soon as they released me, I ran down the stairs and through the kitchen, yanking at the back door. It wouldn't open.

"Stop!" Evie skidded into the kitchen, Andy and Tristan on her heels. She grabbed my arm. "What happened up there?"

I whipped around to face her, tears flowing freely now. "We have to leave," I sobbed. "It's too sad here!" I pulled away from her and wrenched open the door, stumbling down the steps to the back yard. I fought my way through the tangle of weeds and ran across the field to the truck. I fell against it, my lungs protesting the icy night air.

Andy unlocked the door and Tristan helped me climb inside while Andy put the equipment in the toolbox in the bed of the pickup. He got in and ground the engine, turning the heat on full blast.

"We're all here. Let's go." Evie climbed in after me and threw her coat over my lap.

Tristan reached over and started rubbing my hands together in his. "You're freezing, Marissa," he said, concern all over his face. "Why are you so cold?"

I couldn't answer him. I was so overcome with sadness I thought I might never be happy again. It felt like it did the day my mother died and I let the tears fall unabated.

"Is she going to be okay?" Tristan asked Evie.

Evie looked scared. She shoved her black hair off her face and bit her bottom lip. "St. Louis?" She turned my face to hers. "Are you okay?"

I took a shaking breath and nodded. "I think so." I reached up to wipe at my eyes. The truth was, I was absolutely and totally exhausted. Everything in my entire body felt like it had been pulled taut for weeks. "I'm fine," I said, my head leaning over to rest on Tristan's shoulder. "Really, guys. I'm good."

A moment later, the rocking of the truck as Andy wound it along the dark gravel roads lulled me to sleep.

I understand.

CHAPTER 13

"Is she still sleeping?"

"Yeah, let me see that part again."

"Holy cannoli!"

"So strange..."

I woke up in my own room, lying on top of my bed, a quilt thrown over my legs. Someone had taken off my shoes. *How nice*, I thought sleepily, hunkering down into the warmth of my bed and almost dozing off again. *I'm in my room, my friends are here, and nothing happened tonight but a scary dream, right?*

"It really looks like she's talking to someone or something, doesn't it? Show it again."

Evie's voice roused me from my blissful delusion and I sat up straight. I looked over to my television and saw Evie, Andy, and Tristan crowded around. Andy played the footage he took in the Dietrich house.

"There," Tristan said and Andy hit play.

I slid out of bed and crept a bit closer. A movie version of myself walked across an empty bedroom with tattered curtains and faded wallpaper. I looked like I was in a trance. On the screen, I watched myself lean down and put my hand out. Suddenly, I recoiled and the camera jerked. Andy filmed as I looked up horror-struck, my mouth in a silent scream. The camera panned as I fell down, my hands clapped over my ears.

"What the heck?" came Andy's voice on the television. He kept recording as Evie and Tristan ran into the room and lifted me up. A bang behind him made him swing the camera back to the room and the frame held still for a second on a closed door. "Oh my gosh," I could hear Andy whisper before the screen went black.

"Play that again, please?" I asked.

The group on the floor jumped about three feet in the air and turned to look at me. No one said anything for a very long time.

"Play that again, please." I pointed at the screen.

"Go ahead, Andy," said Tristan with a nod. "She deserves to see it."

"Okay," Andy sounded hoarse. He pushed several buttons on the camera and moved the frames to the one he wanted.

I climbed down to the spot on the floor Evie offered me. She took the blanket off her shoulders and wrapped it around mine.

Tristan stared at me.

"What's up?" I asked, suddenly irritated with him.

"Are you feeling all right?" he countered.

"Yeah, a little tired." *And cranky.* I knew I had slept, but I didn't remember falling asleep.

"You passed out about thirty seconds after leaving the Dietrich place," Evie explained.

"Drooled all over Tristan's shoulder." Andy glanced up from the camera. "Seriously, his sweater's soaked."

"Andy, leave her alone."

"Snored like a bear, too."

Evie ignored him. "We couldn't wake you up, so we brought you home, and Andy and I carried you into the house."

"Your dad isn't home yet. He didn't see anything," Tristan added.

"Here it is," Andy said, bringing the video back up on the television screen. The camera swung up from the floor to the ceiling of the landing and then back down again.

I heard Evie's voice: "Andy! Get down here and film." The camera caught footage of Andy's boots and Evie's sneakers as they stood together talking. "She looks really weird. Says she hears music coming from this room."

"Music? Do you think she really hears music?" Andy snorted.

"I don't know, but you know she..."

"Yeah, I know." The camera angle panned up then, and there I was on screen again, my back rigid. Andy stepped around and filmed my face. Tears rimmed my eyes and as I blinked, one escaped. I walked toward the window and Andy swung the camera toward Evie. "What is going on here, Evie?" he whispered.

Evie shook her head. In the background, I can hear my own voice.

"He's crying. He's so sad. H-he wants to know why she left him." I looked possessed as I walked toward the window. I squinted at the television screen, trying to make sense of what I was watching when suddenly, I saw it.

"Look!" I shouted.

Andy nearly dropped the camera.

As he froze the frame, I drew my face up only inches from the flat screen. "Look here," I whispered, pointing.

"What?" Evie asked. Then, she took a sharp breath in. "I see it, too."

"See what?" Tristan and Andy leaned in, almost climbing inside the television. It might have been funny if I hadn't been so scared. Then, at the same instant, they saw it too. Tristan put his hand over his mouth and sat back on his heels.

"That can't be. We can't usually see..." Andy trailed off, looking from the screen to me. The movie was paused and jumping a bit, but you could still see it clearly between jumps. There, in the dark window next to me, was the reflection of an old man's face. He had crazy hair sticking out around his ears and tears were streaming down his face.

I felt icy chills go through me and pulled the blanket around my shoulders again. "Everyone believe me now?" I attempted a nervous laugh. I got up and started to walk toward the door. "I'm going to make some hot chocolate and let this all settle in for a minute. Anyone want to come with me?" I didn't think anyone really wanted to be alone at that moment, and wasn't surprised to hear three pairs of feet following me down the wooden stairs.

I decided on *real* hot chocolate this time and got a copper bottomed pan from the hook above the stove. While the milk was heating, Evie finally broke the silence. "So why is St. Louis the only one who could see him while we were there? We didn't see anything, well, until now. Sorry about that." She nodded at me.

"You know," said Tristan, "I read about a man in New York who believed he could see spirits. He sort of helped these ghosts along to get to the other side."

"How?" Andy pulled four mugs out of the cabinet.

"Well, he would go into a place that someone claimed was haunted and he would try to commune with the ghosts. When he came into contact with the spirit, he would find out why they were still hanging around and then help them fix whatever it was they needed to move on." Tristan shrugged. "I thought it was pretty interesting."

"It still doesn't explain why only Marissa can see these things. Remember the first night in the cemetery? The only one who heard or saw anything while we were there was Marissa. You got any marshmallows?" Andy asked as I poured the steaming chocolate into cups.

"Maybe it's because she was touched by death."

Evie's comment was met with silence around the table.

"I was able to see things before my mom passed away," I said, sitting down and drawing my legs up in the chair. "So, I don't think that's it."

"Did your mom ever talk about seeing anything? It's supposed to be passed down from the mother." Tristan said by way of explanation.

I shook my head. "I don't think so." But, then, I cocked my head to the side. "She did tell me that right before her mom passed away that my grandma came to her one night. Mom was sleeping and she woke up when the bed sank down. You know, like someone was sitting down. She said she thought it was me, that maybe I'd had a nightmare or something, but when she opened her eyes, her mother was sitting there. She told my mom she was okay and that she was happy."

"She wasn't dead yet?" Andy asked.

Tristan rolled his eyes. "Sensitive."

I shook my head again. "No, she didn't pass away until about a week later. Mom said she was completely unresponsive, though."

"So maybe your grandmother was communicating with your mom through some sort of astral projection?" Tristan bit his lower lip. "I mean, it stands to reason, doesn't it? If a ghost is a soul without a body, it makes sense that someone could be a ghost even if they're alive."

"Maybe. My mom said that my grandma never woke up. She passed away and was gone." I swallowed. "The night she visited my mom, she told her that she didn't have to worry about her anymore."

Evie stared across the table at me. "But, you've never seen your mom, have you?"

I wrapped my hands around my mug, the steam rising up. I shook my head.

Tristan reached out and placed his hand on my shoulder. "She's okay, Marissa."

I shrugged. "I know. I just wish I knew for sure."

We sat around sipping hot chocolate, the mood heavy.

"We could try to help him, you know," Andy said.

"Old Man Dietrich? How?" Evie used her finger to stick a marshmallow.

"Marissa could communicate with him," Tristan offered.

I shook my head. "He was so angry."

Evie stuck her finger in her mouth and sucked off the marshmallow. "Sometimes fear and sadness come across as anger."

Tristan pulled out his phone. He swiped the screen and pulled up a page of text. "I found this blog a few months ago and it talks about how to help a loved one move on. This lady wrote it after a family member got trapped."

"How did they get *trapped?*" I asked.

"Her uncle killed himself. He needed forgiveness to move on. But, in other instances, the person doesn't know they're dead, or they have unfinished business."

"Do you think Theodore knows he's dead?" Evie asked.

I looked up at her. "Yeah, I think he knows." The sadness in Theodore's eyes pulled at something in my soul. My eyes filled with tears. "He wants to find Greta and she's *right there.* I don't know why he can't see her."

"Maybe he feels guilty. Maybe he feels like he doesn't deserve happiness anymore." Tristan said.

"But," Evie's voice was small, "everyone deserves happiness, don't they?"

"The auction's next weekend. If we're going to do it, we'll have to go out there sometime this week." Andy got up to rinse out his mug.

"Dad leaves on Tuesday for St. Louis."

"Sounds like it's Tuesday, then. Tristan, what do we need before we go out there again?"

Tristan scrolled through the blog post. "It sounds like we just need to talk to him, tell him that we forgive him."

"Sounds simple enough. I need to head home. Come on, I'll give you a ride."

Tristan put his phone away and stood up. "'Night, ladies, see you at school tomorrow."

I let them out the back door and watched while they drove away in Andy's truck. Then, I rinsed out the rest of the mugs and put them in the dishwasher. Evie sat at the table, her head resting in her hands.

"You okay?" I asked, using a wet washcloth to wipe down the table.

She nodded. "Yeah, I was just thinking about forgiveness."

"Your mom?"

"Yeah, I wonder if she's okay."

"You could call her."

"I could." Evie stared at her phone on the table. She grabbed it and shoved it in the pocket of her jeans. "It's better if I don't, though."

I watched as Evie crossed the room and climbed the stairs. Forgiveness was a hard thing to wrap my brain around. I flipped off the light and followed her upstairs.

Later that night, after tossing and turning for hours, I finally got up and flipped on my desk lamp.

Pulling out a piece of paper and a pencil, I closed my eyes and started to draw.

CHAPTER 14

The house looked even more imposing than the last time we had been out here, if that was possible. I climbed out of Andy's truck and stood staring at it. The moon was hidden behind a thick layer of clouds and I shivered, wrapping my jacket around me.

"You ready?" Tristan asked.

I nodded.

"Let's go." Andy led the way through the field and around the house to the back door. He used the key to open it again and we all stood in the kitchen, barely breathing.

"Is he here?" Evie whispered.

Music wafted down the stairs and sadness crept into my soul. I nodded. "Yeah, he's here. You guys will watch me, right? You won't let anything happen to me?"

"We got you, girl," Andy said, unwrapping his backpack from his shoulders and unzipping it. He handed out flashlights and pulled the camera out of the bag. "Locked and loaded," he said, pushing record.

"We'll be right here the whole time," Tristan assured me. "You lead the way."

My core shuddered and I started up the stairs, my feet resting lightly on the treads. I crested the landing and found myself facing the hallway. It stretched out in front of me and I heard the music blaring, the upbeat tune casting an ominous cadence to my journey to the bedroom door. I placed my hand on the doorknob and turned to see Evie, Tristan, and Andy crowded into the small space behind me. Tristan nodded at me and I felt the doorknob turning in my hand on its own volition.

The scene was the same. The old man, his back to me, the shotgun gleaming in the light cast by the figure at the window. The sadness overwhelmed me for a moment and I felt Evie grab my arm to support me. She stayed by my side as I walked, stiff-legged to the man. I tried to block out the music as it swelled, amplifying the pain and regret swirling around me in the room. I came around to face the man and Evie let go of my arm as I knelt down in front of him.

Tears poured from his eyes and he stared out the window. "Where's my Greta? Where is she?" His voice cracked and my eyes filled with tears.

"Mr. Dietrich?" I said. "My name is Marissa Anderson and these are my friends. We are here to help you."

There was a momentary pause in the music and the atmosphere crackled. Anger welled up from a central point near his feet and spiraled up, jetting from his mouth in a scream. I reached out and placed my hand on his as it lay on the shotgun. "Mr. Dietrich, I need you to listen to me. I know you can hear me if you listen." Tears were pouring from my own eyes now as I listened to him scream.

"Get out! Leave me alone!" Then, another layer to his screaming, like a second voice winding its way up, insistent on being heard. "I'm lonely and scared. Please help me."

The scene in front of me wavered and started to go dark around the edges. I closed my eyes and centered myself. When I opened them again, Theodore had stopped screaming and he was peering at me through cloudy eyes. He leaned toward me and squinted. "I can see you. And I can hear you." His mouth didn't move.

I can see you. And I can hear you, too.

He nodded and his weathered hand grasped mine, a whisper of a touch. "I miss her so much."

It's okay. I understand. She does, too. She forgives you, Mr. Dietrich.

He shook his head slowly. "I did a bad thing."

It's okay. You don't have to be sorry anymore. I took a ragged breath, my eyes rolling back in my head. It was taking so much effort just to stay awake. I focused my energy on the window behind me.

"What is she doing?" Andy's voice was barely a whisper.

"Shhh," Evie said.

She's there. Greta's there. Do you see her?

Theodore's eyes left my face and he looked up over my head. He took a breath and his mouth hung open in disbelief. His eyes gleamed. "I see her. My Greta. Oh, my Greta."

The music tempered and the house grew quiet.

"I'm so sorry, Greta. I wasn't strong enough without you."

She knows. She misses you, too. You can go to her. I swallowed. *It's okay to let go, Mr. Dietrich.*

He looked at me again, his features lightening, the deep wrinkles on his face fading as I watched. He nodded at me and stood up, the shotgun falling from his lap. It landed on the floor with a deafening thud. Theodore looked down at it and then up at me. "It was so heavy."

I nodded. *I know. You can go now.*

He took a shuffling step and then another toward the window. "My Greta, you're so beautiful."

I turned.

Greta stood on the other side of the window. The pane of glass shimmered as she reached through it and extended her hand toward Theodore. "Come, my love, there's a beautiful garden here. We can dance, like we used to."

As he took her hand, the years fell away from his face. The stoop in his back was gone and his hair was dark, slicked back on his head. His eyes were bright and he smiled as he gathered Greta in his arms, swinging her around and around as they faded away.

The music stopped and the shotgun at my feet disappeared. A lightness spread through the room with a sonic boom and I fell back, every fiber of my being exhausted. "It's done," I said. My eyes closed and I slept.

"Did you see anything?"

"Huh uh. You?"

"No, I'll check the camera, but I don't think I caught anything on it either."

"What do you think it looked like for Marissa?"

"I don't know, but the way she was crying, it was probably something pretty amazing."

"You know," I said, sitting up, "you shouldn't talk about people when you think they're unconscious."

"Are you okay? You were out a really long time this time." Tristan's brow furrowed. "We were getting a little worried."

"Nah." Andy plopped down on the edge of my bed and patted my knee. "I knew you'd be fine. That was pretty cool back there."

"Cool," I let the word swirl around my mouth. I wasn't sure how I would describe what happened at the Dietrich farm tonight, but I didn't think "cool" did it justice. Even though I was bone tired, my insides felt tingly and I couldn't stop smiling. Finally, I nodded. "Yeah, it was pretty cool."

"What was it like tonight?" Tristan sat cross-legged on the futon and leaned over a pillow in his lap.

I related everything I saw that evening in the room.

When I was done, Tristan had tears in his eyes. "Wow."

I felt uncomfortable under both of their gazes and averted my eyes. It was then that I realized Evie wasn't in the room. "Hey, where's Evie?"

"She said she had to get something from her room." Tristan cocked his head. "Speaking of which, she's been gone for a while. I'll check on her."

I turned to Andy when Tristan left the room. "It worked, didn't it? We helped Theodore."

Andy watched me with a careful gaze. "Yeah, I think we helped him. What's on your mind?"

I chewed on my bottom lip. "Can I show you something?"

"Is this going to get weird?"

I laughed. "Shut up." I got up from the bed and retrieved a folder from the shelf above the desk. Evie and Tristan walked in the room as I sat down again. "Sometimes when I can't sleep, I get up and draw these."

I opened the folder and drawing upon drawing filtered out onto my teal bedspread. Andy let out a low whistle as he grabbed one of the pencil drawings. The one he was looking at had a woman in a long white dress standing at a window. She stared out at the branches of an enormous oak tree, tears streaming down her face.

"Who is that, St. Louis?"

"I have a guess, and if you think about it, I'll bet you do, too."

She stared down at the paper and then her eyes widened as realization hit. "Is that Mary?"

I nodded. "I think so."

Tristan looked from Evie to me. "You guys going to fill us in?"

"Where's the book?"

I pointed to the closet and Evie retrieved the book and turned to the page we had read almost a month ago now. She read it aloud. Tristan gasped in all the right places, especially at the part when the Union soldiers took Matthias and hung him right in front of Mary.

"So, where is this place?" Andy thumbed at the torn page.

"It doesn't say, but look at this." Evie pulled out a piece of paper from the back cover and unfolded it. "I did some research while we were out shopping in Chillicothe on Black Friday," she said sheepishly, smoothing out the paper. It was a map. "The lady at the historical society made me a copy when I came in to talk to her. She said that she loves talking about Culvers Grove to just about anyone who will listen. She seemed kind of lonely."

"Can't imagine she sees a lot of people asking about this Podunk little town," Andy snorted.

Evie pointed at a bridge on the map. "The closest I can figure is that the cemetery we investigated on Halloween is near where Mary's farm is supposed to be. Remember, you heard crying and thought you saw something?"

I nodded.

"See here?" she asked, pointing at a bridge on the map near the cemetery. "This says Myrtle Bridge is close to the cemetery. Her house must have been in this area here." Her finger made a wide circle to the northwest of the cemetery. "Do you remember that little place we parked on? I think that was the remains of a driveway or road."

"When does your dad get back?"

"He should be here by Friday night."

"I can get off work for Saturday and we could go look then? It should be easier to find during the daytime." Andy stood up.

"She can't on Saturday. Big wedding date with Grant." Evie spun around in my desk chair. "She might be able to do Sunday. You know; if she isn't too worn out from making out with Prince Charming all night."

I threw a pillow at her. "I'll be fine. We'll meet you out at the cemetery at noon on Sunday."

Tristan and Andy got up, gathering their backpacks and then heading down the stairs. I walked them into the kitchen and opened the back door. "See you at school tomorrow."

"Bye!" Tristan waved and headed down the stairs.

Andy hesitated by the door. He shoved his hands deep in his pockets and looked up at me. "You can't help them all."

I blinked. "I don't know what you mean."

"The ghosts. Some of them can't be helped or *won't* be helped. I just don't want you to feel like you have to help them all."

I swallowed. "I know."

He placed a hand on my shoulder and then walked down the steps.

I watched them leave and then locked the door and headed back upstairs. "What were you doing in your room tonight?" I flopped down on my bed and pulled out my science book.

Evie placed the book and folder of drawings on my desk. She shook her head. "Nothing really."

"You were gone a long time."

"It was stupid."

I looked up from my book. "What?"

Evie shifted from one foot to the other. "I was using the Ouija board."

"By *yourself?*"

She crossed her arms over her chest. "It's not a big deal."

"It is. I don't like that thing and I don't think you should be using it alone. What if you open up some sort of portal or something?"

"He's lonely."

"Sam?"

Evie nodded. "There are others, too. They just want a friend, St. Louis. You can understand that, can't you?"

I closed my eyes. "Of course, I understand, but Evie, these people aren't real. I don't know what they are, but they're not here. I think you should stop."

"Then *you* stop drawing." Her eyes blazed.

I sighed. "Fine, I'll stop drawing and you stop with the board. In fact," I got up and grabbed my can full of pencils from the top of my desk. I shoved them at her, "you take these out of my room so I'm not tempted. Here's all my paper, too."

Evie glared at me. "Don't be stupid."

Anger flared. "No, seriously, take them. I wouldn't want something I can't control to inconvenience you."

"That doesn't make any sense!"

"It doesn't have to. Get out of my room!"

I stood fuming long after Evie had shot me a glare and slammed my door behind her. Part of me felt bad and wanted to apologize as soon as I had taken a deep breath. The other part of me ended up winning out and I sat down on my bed, staring unseeing at the pages of my science book.

Evie was already gone by the time I got up for school the next day. Footprints in the snow on the driveway told me that she had decided to walk. I got ready in record time and headed out, catching up with her a few miles down the road. I pulled over to the shoulder and leaned over to open the passenger door. "Get in."

Evie narrowed her eyes and continued walking. I put my car in park and stepped out into the cold winter morning. The sun had just crested the horizon, but it offered little light and even less warmth. I followed her a few steps. "Seriously, Evie, get in the car. It's freezing out here."

Whipping around to face me, Evie threw her backpack down on the ground and set her feet on either side of it. "You have it all, St. Louis, and you don't even know it!"

I stopped short.

"You have a dad and a boyfriend and you can see ghosts! And, I can't do any of that!"

My blood boiled. "My mom is *dead,* Evie! She's gone and I never get to see her again."

"Aw, poor St. Louis. You know what really sucks?" She didn't wait for an answer. "Your mom didn't have a choice to leave you. She was sick and she had to leave. Mine is healthy as a horse and she gave me up. She gave me up, St. Louis! Just like my dad." Tears poured from Evie's eyes.

I stood there on the side of the road in the early morning light, the steam from my breath hanging on the air, and I realized that I had nothing to say. She was right. I sighed. "What do you want me to say? I'm sorry that your dad left and your mom sucks, Evie, but I'm here. And Andy and Tristan and my dad. As for the seeing ghosts thing, I'd gladly hand that over. I feel like I owe them something now and I don't know what to do with that."

Evie sniffed loudly. A car drove by, the driver straining her neck to stare at the two girls in the snow. "I just want to feel like I matter," Evie finally said. She grabbed her backpack from the ground, chunks of heavy snow falling from its bottom as she made her way to the car and climbed in the passenger side.

I got in and closed the door, cranking up the heat full blast and holding my frozen fingers in front of the vents.

"They all want me to help them." Evie's voice was quiet. "Is that how you feel when you see them?"

I stared out the window for a moment before answering. Then, I nodded. "Yeah, I feel like I *should* help them because I might be the only one who can." I thought of all of the drawings in my closet. "And now I feel like Mary's asking for my help."

Evie nodded her head once, her long hair moving with the motion. "Then, that's what we should do."

We sat side by side looking out the windshield.

"St. Louis?"

"Yeah."

"You wanna get going? You drive like a grandma and we're already late."

CHAPTER 15

That Saturday, Grant picked me up for the wedding during the early afternoon. Dad and Evie stood at the front door, waving as I got in his car, my stomach a bundle of nerves. Grant looked amazing in his khakis and white shirt with a neon yellow bow tie. He wore his worn leather jacket and aviators. I kept sneaking glances up at him while he drove.

"How's school?" I asked as he turned onto the highway.

He shifted and then reached over to hold my hand in one smooth motion. He shrugged. "It's okay. I had finals last week, so I'm home for break now."

I smiled. "It will be nice to see you more now that you're home."

Grant shook his head. "Dad's got me working a ton of hours at the hardware store and Mrs. Kirby hired me again for the season at the flower shop." He sighed. "Maybe if your dad needs help again at the farm, I can see you on the weekends?" His voice sounded hopeful and he squeezed my hand.

I thought of the Ghost Hunters Society. "Yeah, the weekends."

We drove in silence for a while, the tires of his car splashing in the melting snow. The sun had beaten down all afternoon and it was beginning to melt the icy surfaces. Dad had warned me that it was supposed to turn off cold tonight, so we needed to watch for refreezing.

"I filled out an application for KU," Grant said, letting go of my hand to downshift when we reached the exit.

"Oh."

"Does that bother you?"

I thought about it for a moment. "No, it's a good school. You'll be fine there."

He laughed. "I know I'll be fine there. I'm asking about you. How do *you* feel about me applying there?"

I shrugged, trying to play it off cool. "It's not that far, and besides, it's not like I get to see you much now."

He pulled into the church's parking lot. White flower wreaths hung from the mammoth red entry doors. Grant parked the car around the side of the church and turned off the engine.

I gathered my purse and had one hand on the door handle when Grant took my other hand in his. "Marissa?"

I stopped and turned back to look at him.

He took off his aviators and ran a hand through his hair. "I'm asking about Kansas City because I don't know if I want to be that far away from my girlfriend."

A smile broke out on my face. "Seriously? Is that how you're asking me to be your girlfriend?" My stomach flip-flopped when I said the word. "I thought the great Grant Hoffman was supposed to be smoother than that."

He looked down and shook his head. "I thought about it the entire time I was driving home from Trenton." He flashed me a smile. "It really did sound smoother in my head."

"Come on, we don't want to be late." I opened the door and slid my hand from his. My heart was beating a million miles a minute as I got out of the car.

Grant got out and rested his arms on top of his car. He cocked his head. "So you're not giving me an answer then?"

I leaned over to get the gift from the back seat. "We've only been out on one date. I mean, what if you get to know me and can't stand something about me?"

Grant walked around and offered his arm. "I doubt you could ever do something I couldn't stand."

I linked my arm through his and allowed him to walk me up the stairs to the church. "I sing along to old boy band music when I'm alone," I said as he signed the guest book.

"Backstreet Boys or N'Sync?"

"Both."

He chuckled as the usher led us down the aisle. When we were seated, he took my hand and held it, his thumb rubbing the top of mine.

I leaned into his side. "I chew ice. And, spit it."

He stared straight ahead, but raised an eyebrow. The music began and a hush fell over the sanctuary.

"Twelve feet's my record," I whispered as the pastor walked to the front of the church.

Grant leaned over and whispered, his warm breath tingling against my ear and neck. "I'm the unmitigated champion of ice spitting this side of the Mississippi. You're on, Anderson."

After the ceremony, the crowd moved down to the basement of the church for the reception. Grant walked me around and introduced me to his entire family and we sat with his mom, dad, aunt and uncle while we ate cake and drank punch. His dad was telling a story about the time he had caught his brother stealing candy from his mom's purse when I realized that Grant wasn't at the table anymore. My brow furrowed as I looked around the room. I finally spotted him near the door that led up and out to the garden area behind the church.

He caught my eye and held up two cups of ice. Wiggling his eyebrows at me, he opened the door and slid through.

A moment later, I excused myself from the table and followed Grant. Upstairs, I slipped out the door into the cool afternoon. The sun hit the brick wall of the church, warming the small enclosed garden and bathing it in a golden light.

"Grant?" I whispered.

A pinging sound and a droplet of water hit my arm as a piece of ice ricocheted off the brick and flew past me into the dark earth at my feet. I turned around, my hand on my hip. "Weak," I said.

Grant stepped from around the corner and handed me a cup. "Show me up, then."

We sat down on the wrought iron bench and took turns trying to hit the trunk of the cherry tree in the center of the garden. He hit it twelve times. I hit it fifteen.

I wiped at my lips with the back of my hand. "My mouth's frozen!"

"I can help that," he said, taking my face in his hands. He leaned in and his lips brushed mine, the scent of his cologne wrapping around me.

I closed my eyes and kissed him back.

"Ahem."

We both jumped at the voice behind us. Grant stood up and pulled me to my feet.

The pastor stood at the doorway. "They asked me to find you for pictures," he said, smiling.

"Oh, sure," Grant said, his ears turning bright red. "Thanks."

The pastor turned and left, and Grant and I barely made it through the photo session without laughing.

When he dropped me off that evening at my house, he stopped the car in the driveway and leaned over the middle console. "The fact that you shamed my ice spitting game aside, I would still like you to consider being my girlfriend."

I smiled and kissed him on the cheek. "Give it another date. You're on a roll."

With that, I stepped out of the car and closed the door behind me. I waved as he drove away and then climbed the steps to the screened in porch. My hand was on the back door when a voice came out of the darkness.

"Hey, St. Louis."

I jumped, my hands flying up in a defensive move that made me feel like a ninja but probably look like a drunk chicken. "Crap, Evie! You scared me! What are you doing out here?"

Evie was wrapped in a quilt, and folded up on a wicker chair on the porch in the dark. I walked over and sat in a chair next to her. It creaked beneath me as I settled into the cushion.

"How was your date?"

"He asked me to be his girlfriend."

"Rough life."

I rolled my eyes. *What was with her?* "Whatever." I started to stand up.

"Wait, don't leave." She looked up at me with wide eyes. "I don't want to be alone right now."

I sat back down, wrapping my jacket around me more tightly. The sun took with it any warmth from earlier in the day when evening came. "What's up with you lately? I thought we were good after the other morning."

Evie sighed heavily. "We're good. I just feel..." she paused. "I feel like after you came to Culvers Grove, everything changed."

My hackles rose. "Well, I'm sorry I came here and ruined everything. It wasn't like I chose to come here, you know."

Evie shook her head. "I know you didn't and I don't mean that you made things worse, either. You just made them different."

"Worse different or better different?"

"For the most part, better different, but something's changed, St. Louis, and I can't quite put my finger on it. It feels like the air has shifted. Like it's more charged somehow."

"That makes absolutely no sense. We would have heard about an electromagnetic wave or a solar storm. We haven't even had a lightning storm in a month."

Evie stood up, her blanket wrapped around her. "I don't know how to explain it. It's like I'm waiting for something to happen, and until then, I feel uncomfortable in my own skin." She shook her head. "It's weird."

"Certifiable."

"Shut it, St. Louis." She gazed at me for a moment, and when she spoke, her voice was lighter. "You hungry? Your dad made spaghetti."

"He cooked?" I stopped short, my mouth hanging open.

"Cooked is such a generous term for what he did. The noodles were crunchy, but he tried." Evie turned toward me, the light from the open door falling across her features. She looked tired and worried in that moment, but then she smiled and the look was gone. I followed her into the house and closed the door behind me.

Had I known what was lurking out there in the darkness of Culvers Grove, I would have locked the deadbolt as well.

CHAPTER 16

"Cheese and crackers! There's nothing but mud out here!" Tristan pulled his foot from a puddle, the mud settling back into the hole with a squelching protest.

"What do you expect? It's been nothing but melting snow for three days now!" Andy slid down the hill sideways, as if he was riding a snowboard.

"Show off."

"We're never going to find Mary's house with you two arguing." Evie looked positively miserable in jeans with mud up to the knees.

"Hate to break it to you, Patton, but our love spat has nothing to do with us not finding the house. I think it's your poor map reading skills there, Magellan."

Evie flipped Andy off and stalked back down the hill toward his truck. It was parked just off the road near the cemetery. We had spent the last three hours fighting our way through mud and tangled grass trying to find the road that led to Mary's house. We had ended up following the road Evie and I originally thought might lead to her house for about a half mile before it ended unspectacularly into a creek swollen with three days' worth of melted snow. It didn't look like the road continued on the other side, so we turned back.

Andy looked at the three of us as we stood outside his truck. He shook his head. "No way are any of you getting in Lucille."

"*Lucille?*" Evie snorted.

"Huh uh, I'd never get that amount of mud cleaned out of her."

Tristan pulled a set of keys from his pocket and dangled them in the air. "Too bad he forgot that he gave me a key to his sweet ride." He grinned deviously and hit the key fob. The lights on the truck lit up twice and the horn sounded.

Before Andy could get his keys from his pocket, Evie, Tristan, and I had piled in, turning to look at Andy expectantly.

He stared at us for a minute and then dropped his head, shaking it. Without a word, he climbed in next to us and turned the engine over. "You're all helping me clean her when we get back to town."

"We're sorry, Lucille," we sang on the way.

I looked over at Evie. She was staring out the window, lost in thought. I nudged her side. "You okay?"

She nodded but kept looking out the window.

I nudged her again. "We'll try again soon."

The last few days of school flew by before break. Teachers seemed distracted and students were rowdy. After the warmup, the winter took hold by its teeth, sending the mercury plummeting and dropping a foot and a half of snow on the ground. Dad had returned from St. Louis and planned to stay home through the New Year. He'd been shut up in his office for days now, working on a case and had only come out to refill his coffee cup. In fact, between him working, me drawing picture after picture of Mary and texting and talking to Grant on his breaks, and Evie doing whatever she was doing in her room with the Ouija board, we hadn't been in the same room to have a conversation in weeks. I missed my friend, but the door opened both ways, and I was tired of apologizing for things I couldn't change.

Jessica caught up with me on the last day of school before break in front of my locker. "Hello, stranger!" She leaned up against the bank of lockers. "Listen, I haven't seen you around in, like, forever so I haven't had a chance to invite you over to my parent's house for Christmas. Rick invited half the football team and some of his friends from college. It's going to be the same crew that was at Laura's party. I know you had to leave early because of your allergies and I thought you might like to get to know them because they're really cool people. My parents had planned on a small dinner, but at this point, it's kinda become a Christmas shindig and they told me to invite who I wanted. The more the merrier!"

It sounds like a nightmare. I closed my locker and looked at her. "I don't think I can make it."

"You can bring your dad, too. And, those other friends of yours," she added quickly when I didn't say anything.

"No, it's not that," I said softly.

"Well, then, do you have other plans?" Jessica was beginning to look hurt and I hated when she looked like that.

"I'm sorry. It's just that we were going to spend a quiet holiday on the farm. I appreciate the offer, though."

Jessica looked down at the gray and black tiles. "Oh, well, if you decide later that you want to come, let me know."

I'd rather pull my eyebrows out with duct tape. "Thanks," I mumbled. I put my head down and headed to Chemistry. A few minutes later, I was busy trying to yank my book out of my backpack when I heard a tapping on the window next to me. I looked over and gasped. "What are you doing here?" I hissed.

Grant shot me a smile and jerked a thumb at the door.

I launched my hand into the air. "Ms. Creavy?"

"Yes, Marissa?"

"May I be excused? I really need to use the restroom."

"Go ahead. Everyone else, get out your books and turn to page one-oh-two." Her voice faded away as I made my way out the door and to a side entrance of the building near the restrooms. It opened to a small inset that led out to the back of the school. During warmer weather, the PE class used the exit to get to the track, but the door was forgotten during the winter. Snow had drifted into the corner, a couple feet deep underneath the outcropping of concrete over the entryway. I opened the heavy door and stuck a rock between it and the threshold to keep it from locking behind me. Grant stood leaning against the red brick of the building.

"What on earth is so important?" The wind whipped around the space, caught in an eddy of frigidness. "You know I could get detention for this, right?"

He looked up and smiled. "Aw, come on," he pushed away from the wall, "no one would give you detention this close to the holidays." He looked down at me. "You look beautiful today," he said as he kissed me.

I've watched enough movies in my life to know that the term "time stopped while we kissed" was about the oldest and cheesiest way to describe a kiss, but that's exactly how I felt. The cold went away and there was nothing in that second. It was only Grant and I in the entire world.

A moment later, he stepped away and smiled at me again.

I opened my eyes slowly, realizing that the smell of his cologne would be with me the rest of the day. The thought made me almost giddy.

He took off his leather jacket. "Here, you're cold." He wrapped it around me with arms still holding onto the almost forgotten summer's tan.

"I know you didn't come here just to do that," I said, my cheeks flushing. *Although I'm really glad you did.*

"I have to get back to the hardware store soon." He jerked his head over his shoulder. "Dad said I could have a few minutes. I had to give this to you." Grant held out a small package to me.

"What's this?"

"A Christmas present, goofball," he said. "Open it."

I smiled and looked down at the gift. With trembling hands, I pulled at the ribbon and paper. Inside was a little felt box in the shape of a heart. I looked up at him with a raised eyebrow.

"I know," he grinned sheepishly, "but it was the only box they had at the store. Open it!"

I popped open the box and inside was a small gold pendant. It was a sun with a crescent moon wrapped around it. "I love it. Thank you." I gave him a hug and a kiss on his neck.

"I thought of you when I saw it."

"Really? Why?"

"Okay, now don't make fun. Promise?" His brow furrowed.

"I promise." *I don't.*

"It reminded me of you because...never mind. It sounded better when I said it on the way over here. Now it just sounds goofy." Grant looked down and shuffled his feet, hands jabbed deep into his pockets.

I took a step closer and wrapped my arms around his middle. "Tell me," I whispered.

He leaned down and kissed the top of my head. "Fine, it reminds me of you because I think about you night and day," he said quietly into my hair. "I really like you, Marissa."

"And I really like you, too."

He leaned down and kissed me again.

"Hey!" said a voice behind us.

I whirled around and came face to face with the custodian.

"This isn't allowed." He pointed to the rock I had jammed in the space.

"I'm, um, sorry. I have to go," I gave Grant a peck on the cheek and headed back into the building.

"I'll text you later," he said.

When I returned to class, Ms. Creavy was in the midst of her lecture on stoichiometry. I pulled out my tablet and started taking notes. *It* would *be her that taught until the very last minute of school.* I sighed.

My phone buzzed in my pocket and I pulled it out, swiping at the screen as I held it under the table. I glanced up. Ms. Creavy had her back turned. I looked down at my phone. It was a message from Grant. *First clue is in the box. Text me your answer.*

I glanced up again. I pulled the velvet box out of his jacket pocket and opened it under the table. I ran my finger over the smooth face of the sun and moon and smiled. On the top was a folded piece of paper. I unfolded it and read the handwritten message: *What's the first name of the person who played Buddy the Elf?*

I texted. *Will.*

A moment later, my phone buzzed and I looked down. It was a screenshot of a bottle of cologne. I texted back. *Hugo?*

I took notes for a while and then my phone buzzed again. *Sorry, got busy. If I was the gingerbread man, what did the fox do?*

Ate me?

Aha, no.

Tricked me?

No.

I bit my bottom lip. *Outwitted me?*

Yeah, now put it all together.

The bell rang and everyone gathered their things and headed toward the door. I looked at my texts and put them together, pressing send.

A moment later, the text came back. *Of course, I will! I thought you'd never ask.*

I furrowed my brow. Then, it dawned on me. *Omg. That was adorable.*

As soon as class let out, I rushed to the cafeteria to talk to my friends. I bought a can of soda from the machine and shoved it in my backpack. I wasn't really hungry today. My stomach was in excited knots. I had played it cool, but going out with Grant was just about perfect. No one was sitting outside, so I jogged down to the Art room. Andy and Tristan were eating lunch at a desk together and they looked up when I walked in.

"Oh," Tristan said, sounding disappointed. "We thought maybe Evie was with you."

"Where is she?" I put my backpack down on one of the desks.

"She got called out of Civics last period," Andy said around a giant mouthful of sandwich. Tristan rolled his eyes and handed him a napkin.

"What for?" I asked.

"Dunno," Andy said.

Something's wrong. "I'm going to check with the office." I walked up the stairs, my pace quickening when I heard Evie's voice.

"I'm not going!" she shouted.

I rounded the corner and saw Evie standing in the office doorway, her mom staring her down a foot away.

"Evie, what's going on?"

Her mother turned and looked at me, her eyes narrowing. "You!" she snarled. "You and your lawyer daddy think you can come along and take my baby girl? We was just fine before you!" Her teeth were yellow and I could smell a strong odor of alcohol teeming off her.

I glanced over at Evie who looked like she would crawl under the carpet if she could find a loose corner. "Ms. Patton," I started as calmly as I could. "Listen, I know you're upset..."

"Upset?" she screamed, her bloodshot eyes rolling to the ceiling and back down again. "I'm way beyond upset, little girl!"

Mr. Jameson came out of his office and quickly scanned the situation. "What seems to be the problem here?"

Evie's mom whirled around on him. "This little witch and her father are tryin' to take away my Evie! And, I've come to get her back! Now come on!"

She tried to grab Evie's elbow, but Evie shrugged her off. Ms. Patton reached out with a hand and slapped Evie across the face, the sound echoing in the quiet hallway. Evie whimpered and she dropped her head, black curls hiding her face from view.

I froze.

"Now, Ms. Patton," the principal said, sugar dripping from his voice as he positioned himself in between Evie and her mother. "I can't have you coming in here and hitting my students."

"But she's my daughter!" Evie's mom wailed. The noise was beginning to draw a crowd. Several students had stopped to watch, mouths hanging open.

My heart ached for Evie.

"I understand that, Ms. Patton," Mr. Jameson kept speaking softly and slowly, taking Evie's mom by the arm and beginning to walk her toward the door of his office. "But, this is school property and my job is to keep my students safe. I'm sure you understand, right? Now, let's get you a seat here in my office. Betty," he motioned for the secretary, "perhaps you can get Ms. Patton here a cup of strong black coffee?"

Evie's mom turned to glare at me from the doorway. "This isn't over!" she hissed. Mr. Jameson closed the door before she could say anything else.

"Oh, Evie," I cried, running over to her and putting my arms around her. "Are you okay?"

"No," came the small voice. "No, I'm not okay. This is not okay!" She looked up wildly at all of the faces peering at her from the panes of glass surrounding the office. "This is not okay!" she shouted, breaking from me and running down the hallway.

I stood there for a full minute, watching the crowd finally disperse.

I felt a hand on my shoulder. The secretary was looking at me kindly, steaming cup of coffee in her other hand. "I've called your father. He's on his way." She smiled and patted me on the shoulder and opened the door of Mr. Jameson's office, handing in the coffee. "I'll be happy to call a cab for Ms. Patton," she said as I left the office to find Evie.

After looking in most of her regular places, I finally found her in the library, tucked away in the back shelves near the conference rooms. She was folded into a small ball, sobbing.

I sat down next to her quietly, listening to her cry. "My dad's on his way."

She looked up, her eyes red and tears streaming down her cheeks. One cheek bore a spider web of purple broken blood vessels where her mother had hit her. I pulled the cold can of soda from my back-pack and handed it to her. She put it on her face and attempted a smile.

"Think I'll win most popular this year in the year-book?" She winced as she held the can to her face.

"No." I looked up at the shelves of books. "Probably more like biggest scene maker."

She laughed a little at that one. "This sucks, St. Louis. What is wrong with her? Seriously? Who would do that to their own kid?"

Since I didn't have an answer, I just sat next to her until she finally stopped crying and handed the can of soda back to me.

She dropped her head onto my shoulder and sighed. "Do you think your dad would agree to stopping for ice cream on the way home?"

"I'm pretty sure you can talk him into it," I said. "You want to go see if he's here yet?" She nodded and we walked upstairs, ignoring the whispers as we walked down the hall.

"This will be all over school by the end of the day," Evie groaned.

"Nothing you can do about that now," I said.

"Gee, thanks."

"No, I mean, you can't do anything about what happened. People will talk, but people will also forget. Just give it time."

"You know," she said gravely, "I wish you were right, St. Louis, but unfortunately, memories are much, much longer in a small town."

When we got to the office, my dad was talking with the principal. We stood quietly in the corner until he noticed us.

He strode over and looked at Evie's face. "Are you okay?"

We nodded and Evie looked dangerously close to crying again. Dad put his arm around her shoulders. "If we're done here?" he asked the principal.

"Yes, Mr. Anderson. I'll excuse the girls for the rest of the day."

"Thank you." Dad guided Evie out into his waiting truck. I followed behind with both of our backpacks. I got in and scooted to the middle and Evie climbed in behind me. Dad closed her door and walked around the front of the truck, pulling a candy from his pocket. The crow's feet had deepened around his eyes in the last few months.

"Hey, Mr. A?" Evie said as we pulled out of the parking lot.

"Yes, Genevieve?"

"Can we stop for ice cream?"

"A perfectly reasonable request when there's a foot of snow on the ground and the wind chill is twelve below." He smiled and looked over at her.

I reached up and put my hand on his arm. "Thanks, Dad," I whispered.

He smiled at me in the mirror and turned off to head up the highway to the McDonalds in Eagleton. The lady at the window looked at us strangely, as she handed us three ice cream cones wrapped in a napkin. Dad paid and we were on our way, Christmas carols playing on the radio.

Up until the scene in the office, this had been almost a perfect day for me. I reached inside my pocket and ran my fingers over the felt box, thinking of the gold chain from my mother that I would wear the pendant on.

"And, little miss," Dad said, eyeing me as he waited for the one light in town to change. "I'm assuming this jacket you showed up in has an owner?"

I smiled. "I'll tell you all about it later, Dad."

That night, while Evie was doing homework in her room and Dad was on the phone, I sat back in my chair and looked up at the photo I had taken of Grant driving my dad's tractor. Mom would have really liked him. Yeah, I decided, he was pretty handsome. And smart. And a little bit romantic. I pulled out my phone and played the song that we danced to at his cousin's wedding. I grabbed his jacket from the back of my desk chair and held it up to my face, breathing deeply of the scent of leather and his cologne as I sat down on my bed.

"Good Lord," came Evie's voice from the doorway, "don't you have any shame, St. Louis?"

I threw the coat down and swiped at the screen of my phone, feeling my face flush. "Don't you knock?"

The redness had gone away on Evie's face. She closed the door behind her and walked over to sit down on the futon, pulling her legs up in front of her and placing a pillow in her lap. She leaned on it and looked at me. "Tell me more about your mom?"

"What do you want to know?"

"Well, before she got...sick. What did you guys used to do together?"

I sighed, and then smiled. "We did a lot of laughing and talking. She was always really nosy, but in a nice way. She wanted to know my friends and what went on at school. She also liked animals. She went to vet school for a semester before she met my dad. Then, she got into the insurance business and never got back to vet school. She always told me she wanted a hundred acres and twelve horses, a cow, and a goat."

"Did she ever get any of that?"

I shook my head. "No, but she said that all of that didn't matter because she had the things that really counted in her life."

"I wish I'd gotten to meet her, St. Louis."

There was a soft knock at the door. "Can I come in?"

I got up and opened the door. Dad was standing outside in a red flannel shirt. He raked a hand through his graying hair and sat down at my desk.

"Genevieve, we need to talk about what happened today with your mom and what we can do to make sure it never happens again. My friend is ready to file a personal protection order for you on my word. What that means is if we decide to file, your mom will have no contact with you. Here, at school, when you're out in town," he ticked them off on his fingers. "She will be legally required to keep away from you."

Evie stared at my dad and then at me. A smile broke out on her face. "All I have to do is say that I want this?"

Dad kept his voice level and slow. "It's completely up to you, Genevieve. I want you to understand the severity of this, okay?"

"I understand, Mr. Anderson, and I want to file. I don't ever want her near me again."

"Okay, I'll let Pat know. He'll have it pushed through the courts by this weekend."

"Thanks. You know, for everything."

"No worries." Dad stood up and walked to the door. "I'm sorry that happened to you today, dear. It shouldn't have happened, and I'm, well, I'm sorry it did." He closed the door behind him.

"What's your mom going to do?" I asked when I heard my dad's bedroom door close downstairs. "When she hears you have an order against her, I mean."

Evie set her jaw. "She doesn't get to do anything. As soon as she signed away guardianship, she gave up any right to do anything to me."

I raised my eyebrows.

"I'm not stupid, St. Louis. I heard you and your dad talking about how she left the papers in the door."

I sat there for a minute, rolling different things around in my head to say. None of them seemed to fit, though. "Are we okay?" I finally asked.

Evie pulled her long hair over her shoulder. She looked out the window as she played with the ends of her hair. "I don't know what's wrong with me lately. I thought maybe it had to do with my mom and all the drama we're going through, but it seems like more."

"I think it might be the board."

Her eyes blazed. "It's not the board! Besides, it's broken."

I cocked my head to the side.

"Yeah, it's only been spelling one word over and over again." She shrugged.

"What word?"

"It's nonsense. G-I-S-A."

I searched it on my phone. "The Georgia Independent School Association?"

Evie smiled. "I doubt it."

I scrolled through the rest of the results and didn't come up with anything else that would fit. "Are they asking for help anymore?"

Evie shook her head. "Not like I could help them anyway. It was stupid."

I sat quietly for a moment. "There is one person we could try to help."

"I thought *I* was your pet project these days. Giving up?"

"Shut up. I was talking about Mary."

Evie shrugged. "We still don't know where her house is."

"Want to go look tomorrow again? I'll get Dad to take us to pick up my car from school and then we can go look."

She brightened. "Yeah, we can go again." She stood up. "I'm going to go take a shower. Night."

"Night."

She closed the door behind her and I heard the water in the bathroom turn on. I changed into my pajamas and walked over to my desk. I stared at the journal for a long time before finally pulling it off the shelf and sitting down on my bed. I had been thinking all afternoon about how different my mom had been from Evie's. And how lucky I was to have had a mom like that. I opened the book to about the halfway point and smiled at all of the memories I had added over the last few months.

Mom: I wanted to say thank you. Thank you for everything you were to me. You were my friend, my confidant, my mom. I know that you're gone, but I wanted you to know that I loved you, love you, and will always love you. And, I'm glad that you were my mom, if only for a little while.

I closed the notebook and sat for a minute, rubbing my hand over the cover. Hot tears stung my eyes and I blinked several times. It wasn't fair. It really wasn't and I felt myself getting angry. *Why did she have to leave? She was the best mom in the world and had so much love to give and we had so much left to do together.* I sat there for a minute and lost myself in the anger. I dug my fingernails into the palms of my hands and let the tears roll down my cheeks. I focused on the white ball of rage inside my chest and let it hurt all the way down to my toes, letting it radiate through my body. I was mad at the doctors who lied to me, the cancer for taking my mom away, my friends for abandoning me, my dad for moving me to the middle of nowhere, and my mom for dying. As unfair as I knew it was, I was mad at her for leaving us. She should have fought harder. She should have stayed around. She should have been okay. Sobs wracked my body and I took deep breaths, sucking in cool air with giant gulps. Slowly, the anger faded and I knew. I knew she was gone and that none of this was her fault.

And, maybe most importantly, I finally knew that none of this was *my* fault either.

I also knew why I hadn't seen my mom since she died and I finally understood that this was a good thing. She had moved on and she was happy. Only ghosts had something left unfinished.

Hugging the notebook to me, I put it back on the shelf, smiling as I did. Calm settled over me and for the first time in a long time, I felt completely at peace.

CHAPTER 17

I crested the hill and spotted Evie ahead. "Did you see it over there?" I panted. It was the first day of winter break and we'd spent most of the late morning trudging around in the snow, trying unsuccessfully to find Mary's house.

"No. You?" Evie fought through the drifts toward me.

"Huh uh, I think we'll have to wait until this clears out a little."

Evie groaned audibly.

"I know," I said as she drew up even with me, "but, we're not going to be able to go deep enough into the woods with all of this snow. Let's call it a day and go get something to eat, okay?"

Evie pouted and I could feel myself getting somewhat frustrated with her. I wanted to find Mary's house just as badly as Evie, but she couldn't argue with the fact that the northern Missouri winter and its snowfall was in full swing. She stood at my car for a minute as I knocked the snow off my boots.

"Do you think we were close?" She rested her chin on the open car door.

"I think we have a long way to go, but we can't do anything until I can drive up that road to get us closer. It's too far to walk in all of this snow."

My car slid a couple of times as I backed out, but then it found traction and we headed to town. I cleared my throat. "The weatherman said last night to expect a big warm-up tomorrow, so the snow shouldn't last too long." I looked at Evie sideways, hoping to make her feel at least a little better. "It's also Christmas Eve in a couple days. And then presents!"

I pulled into a parking space in front of the café on the square and turned off the car. "Bring in the map, Evie, and we'll take a look at it again while we're eating, okay?"

She pulled out the crumpled piece of paper from her backpack.

Sipping on two sodas while we waited for our grilled cheeses and fries, I pointed to a blank space on the map.

"What about that?" I asked. "See how it shows sort of a clearing here? Do you think that could be the house?"

"I don't know." Evie's brow furrowed as she leaned in close over the map. "I guess it could, but I've always thought it would be here, see?" She pointed to a spot on the map about an inch southeast. "I thought it might be there because the cemetery is right there and it's so close to the creek. Your spot is about a half a mile to the northwest."

"I know, but we've looked behind the cemetery and can't find anything, and I don't know about you, but when we were out there, I didn't pay any attention to where that road led. It could have made a turn to the left into the woods at the creek instead of going straight back behind the cemetery. You don't remember, do you?"

Evie shook her head. "No, but I say your idea is worth a try. We didn't see anything today and I think your place is as likely as any. Let's try it tomorrow."

"Yeah, we *could* try it tomorrow," I paused, "but I think we have to go when it's dark, though."

She smiled. "Getting brave, huh?"

I shook my head. "No such luck. The book said that people hear weeping from the bridge when there's a full moon."

Realization dawned on Evie's face. "That's it! You can listen for the sound and lead us right to the house!"

I wasn't nearly as confident as Evie in my abilities, but I thought it was a better option than wandering through the muddy terrain the next day.

Jessica brought over two grilled cheese platters with fries.

"Thanks!" I said. "I didn't know you were working today. The other waitress took our order."

"Yeah, she had an emergency at home so they called me in. I got here a minute ago to take over. How are you guys doing?" She scooted into the booth next to me and grabbed a fry from my plate. "You know," she said, twirling it between her fingers, "I could eat these French fries every day of my life!" She took a bit and smiled. "'Course I would weigh like a million pounds and have to be on the bottom of all the cheerleader pyramids. Oh, what's this? Did your dad give this to you for Christmas? It's really pretty." Jessica reached out to pull my necklace toward her.

"No," I hesitated. I wasn't quite sure how public Grant wanted our relationship. And, in a town as small as Culvers Grove, you'd better be sure you were ready for everyone to know when you told that first person. I swallowed. "It's from Grant."

"Grant Hoffman?" Jessica breathed, wide-eyed. She held up the pendant and turned it in her hand. "Wow, my friend Casey dated him for a while last year and he never gave her anything like that. Are you guys like," she dropped her voice and leaned forward, "a thing?"

"I guess you could say that."

"Good grief," Evie piped up. "Jessica, you should see them together. They're absolutely enamored with each other. It's quite disgusting, really." She smiled around a French fry.

"I remember what it was like when Rick and I first got together..."

Evie and I shared a secret smile as Jessica launched into a long story about the wonderful things about her boyfriend. Fifteen minutes later, another customer came into the diner and she left us to our own quiet conversation again.

"How did you ever get to be friends with her?" Evie nodded her head back and forth and chomped on pretend gum.

"Leave her alone," I laughed. "She's the first person I met here. And, she means well."

"Whatever," Evie said, rolling her eyes. "Are you ready to go?"

"Yeah," I said, pulling out a twenty and laying it on the table. We got back into the car and started home.

When we got home, Evie headed upstairs to her room. "I'm going to take a shower and get things ready for tonight. You want to put together a bag?"

I nodded and started up the stairs behind her.

"Can you come in here a minute?" Dad called from his office.

"I'll be up later." I walked back down and into Dad's office, flopping down on one of his leather chairs. "How's the lawyer stuff going?"

"It's okay," he said. "I have to head to St. Louis for a few days right after the holidays."

"You'll be here for Christmas?"

He nodded.

"And New Year's?"

"Yeah."

"Okay, then." I said, getting up and starting toward the door. "Evie and I are going out tonight for a little while. Jessica invited us over to watch a movie."

"Can we talk for a minute?" Dad put down the pen he had been writing with and came out from behind his desk.

"Um, sure." I reclaimed my spot on the chair, guilt creating icy tendrils in my arms and legs. I hated lying to him.

Dad cleared off some files and sat down in the other chair, facing me. "I was wondering how things were going." He pulled a candy from his shirt pocket and opened it.

"All right, I guess."

"Okay," he said, "so be more specific and tell me how things are going with Grant."

"They're good," I said.

Dad regarded me as he pulled the wrapper straight between his thumb and finger. "Things getting pretty serious?" he asked.

"I guess." I cleared my throat. "I guess we're girlfriend and boyfriend now." I rolled my eyes inwardly. *That sounded stupid when I said it out loud.* I looked at my dad, who was suddenly looking very uncomfortable and it dawned on me. "Oh, ew, Dad! I'm not talking to you about this!" I stood up.

"Sit down. It'll be fine." His ears turned bright red. He leaned back in his chair, rolling the butterscotch around in his mouth before speaking again. "Well, this was always your mother's department, and as I am entirely too good-looking and young to be a grandfather, I thought we should talk about it."

"Dad," I said, patiently, "Mom gave me all of the information I need, and really, you don't need to worry. I'm not ready for that yet and neither is Grant."

"I know, and I trust you. I want you to be careful and if you need someone to take you to town to get…" Dad looked positively green for a moment.

I looked at my dad, horrified. *Did he really say he would take me to get on the pill?* I took a deep breath. "Dad, if and when I decide to have sex," I watched as he blanched a bit at the word, "I will let you know. In the meantime, know that I'm not ready and I won't be for a while. All right?"

He nodded and then got up to grab his empty coffee cup off the desk. "I'm going to go get some more coffee and pretend I'm comfortable with the conversation we just had. Do you want me to fix you some dinner?"

"No thanks, we ate in town," I said, getting up and walking toward the stairs. I stopped on the first step and turned. "Dad?"

"Yeah, Peanut?"

"I love you."

"I love you, too."

"We are *definitely* finding that house tonight, St. Louis!"

The temperature had dropped again ahead of the warm front and the wind whipped around me, cutting through my clothes like knives. My car was parked just off the road near the cemetery and we walked up the hill away from it. The full moon cast its silvery light over the snow, making it almost glow. I had been afraid the clouds would cover it and we would be fighting our way through the field in the dark. Luck was on our side, though, and the moonlight was bright enough that we hadn't needed to turn on our flashlights since leaving the car.

"There," I said pointing, "see how the ruts turn to the left?" Evie nodded. "Let's follow it and see what we find."

By late evening, we were deep within the woods, canvassing back and forth. The woods were quiet and peaceful. The only sound we heard was the crunching of dry leaves and needles under our boots. The thick canopy above had kept much of the snow from building up and walking was much easier here.

I stopped and listened.

"Hear anything?"

I listened for a moment longer and then shook my head. "No, let's go this way."

Evie had her phone out, the compass app twisting around as we walked. She nodded. "I think you're right."

As I walked, I thought about Mary. Suddenly, I stopped. "What if it's not real?"

Evie almost bumped into me. She looked up from her phone. "What if what's not real?"

"The story about Mary."

She ignored me, instead, taking the map out of her bag and spreading it on the ground. I flipped my flashlight on and focused the beam on it.

"I don't understand," she murmured. "The creek should be right up here. I don't hear any water, though."

I wrapped my arms around my middle. The wind picked up, tossing the branches above us and raining snow down onto our heads.

Evie brushed the map off and placed it back in her bag. She stood up. "Well, what do you want to do?"

I stood for a moment, torn between wanting to get back in my warm car and drive home and staying out here with my friend, looking for a house that probably wasn't even standing anymore. Evie stared hopefully at me and I made up my mind. "Thirty more minutes, then we go home."

She smiled and started walking, her long black hair spilling out from under her knit cap. I sighed and followed. We walked deeper into the woods. Cresting a small hill, Evie stopped and pointed. "There it is! We couldn't hear it because it's frozen solid."

I climbed up the small rise and stood beside her, looking down into the valley. There, cutting through the trees, was a small creek, its water frozen in a solid sheet of ice. "Nice job. Now, which way?"

Evie looked both ways and then considered her phone. She looked up and pointed with a nod of her head. We headed to the left, winding our way closer to the creek as we followed it downstream. My breath hung in the air as we walked silently through the woods.

Evie was several feet in front of me when I heard her say something. I stopped walking. "What?"

She stopped and turned. Shaking her head, she said, "I didn't say anything."

A wind started from somewhere behind us, building as it hurtled toward my feet, carrying with it dead leaves and sparkles of snow. It hit me full force, driving me back a few feet and then whipping past me, before disappearing into the forest beyond the creek. The sound started low and then built, winding its way around the tree trunks, spiraling up to the branches above my head. Tears filled my eyes and I gulped a breath of icy air. It hurt my lungs.

Evie was beside me. "You hear something, don't you?"

I nodded, clamping down on my lips to keep them from quivering.

"Come on," she coaxed, reaching out to take my hand. "Let's walk toward it."

No, let's turn around and walk, no, run, back to the car and forget about this. I nodded and followed the sound, my feet finding the path easily as I walked. The sound of crying began to fill my consciousness, pulling at my soul. I could see Evie, and her mouth was moving, but I couldn't hear what she was saying. The only thing in the woods, in the entire world, was the sound of wailing. I had made the same sound when my mom's casket was lowered into the ground. A small cry escaped as I followed Evie down to the creek.

The sound amplified, filling the forest around us as we stepped from the underbrush. There, to our left, was a bridge. Its wooden slats led across the creek to a hill beyond. Evie stepped onto it, testing it with a gentle jump. She nodded at me and held my hand as I stepped onto the bridge.

The second my feet were planted on the wood, the noise stopped. I stood, the silence shocking. I cleared my throat. "This is it."

Evie nodded and we walked together over the bridge, the frozen wood crisply cracking as our weight settled on it.

Once on the other side, I felt the coldness creep into my body. I shivered. "D-did you hear any of that?"

Evie looked at me, her eyes wide. "No, I didn't hear anything. Was it bad?"

I nodded. "Yeah, it was pretty bad."

We walked together up the rise and wound our way to the top. Suddenly, we happened upon a clearing hidden behind the hill, and Evie and I stopped short at the tree line.

"Whoa," Evie breathed.

Standing before us in the clearing was a house.

"Looks like we found Mary's house, St. Louis."

It was red brick and two stories, five windows lining the second floor. Below was a porch that sagged from the front of the house, its white pillars broken and jutting out of the crumbling porch. Behind the house was a barn and half of a silo still standing. A rock fence ran along the backyard, a tree growing up through the stones, crumbling it in the middle. The side of the house had two windows on bottom and two on top. The windows had long been broken out and the house seemed to be yawning in its clearing. Hanging in the right top window was a lace curtain. This was the only window in which the glass was still intact. I thought I saw the curtain move and turned to say something to Evie, but she was already halfway to the house, picking her way through the deep snow. I caught up with her, the feeling of dread filling me deeper with each step.

"Let's go in," Evie whispered, walking up onto the porch. The wood creaked angrily at her and she peeked through where the front door had stood. She walked through the door and disappeared into the darkness inside. "Come on!" she called.

I stepped carefully up onto the porch and in through the door. "Oh, Evie," I said.

"Be careful," Evie said from the other side of the parlor. "It's really broken down there." She pointed toward the middle of the room where the floor was noticeably dipping. It looked as if it would drop with any weight on it at all. I skirted around the walls toward Evie. Looking up, I could see the ceiling dipping in as well. It was as if the whole house was getting ready to fall in on itself. We crept to the back of the house into what used to be the kitchen.

"Look at this." Evie held up a broken wooden spoon she had picked up from the floor.

There was a flash of bright white light, and suddenly, the kitchen looked sunny and new. A beautiful young woman was standing at a table, holding a large bowl in the crook of her left arm and stirring something inside with the wooden spoon. Her jet black hair was drawn back in a tight bun and she was wearing a calico blue dress with a high neck. She was humming.

Suddenly, there was a knock at the door behind me. I swung around and saw a past version of the parlor, complete with lace curtains and wingback chairs. A fire was crackling warmly in the fireplace. The lady in the kitchen put down her bowl and wiped her hands on her apron.

"Coming!" she called out as she walked into the parlor, stopping to smooth her hair in a mirror on the wall. She opened the door. Outside on the porch stood a man dressed in a tattered gray uniform. He was dirty and thin, with bare feet and a full beard over his gaunt cheeks. He stood up straight and took his hat off, blue eyes twinkling.

"Good evening to you, sir," I heard the woman say guardedly. A flush rose to her alabaster cheeks.

"Ma'am," he said. He attempted to bow in respect but then staggered a bit. He held onto the porch railing. His mouth opened to say something

else and then his eyes rolled up to the top of his head
and he collapsed onto the porch.

Mary stepped forward, looking out toward the
dirt road, which ran in front of the house. Her lips
spread into a thin line and she reached down to take
the man by his shoulders. She pulled him into the
house, the heels of his bare feet dragging behind him.
She retrieved his hat from the porch and looked toward the road once more before closing the door.
The man lay on the floor, his breathing uneven and
labored.

Mary considered him for a moment and then
went to the sideboard in the parlor and pulled a container from inside. Opening it, she held the container
near the man's face.

He flinched away and sat up coughing. When he
got his breath again, he looked up at her, shame
masking his features. "I apologize for my intrusion,
ma'am. My name is Matthias Stratford. I am a soldier returning from the battle at Pea Ridge and I am
simply looking for a hot meal and perhaps a place to
stay for the night in your barn loft before I move on.
That is," he dropped his gaze, "if the man of the
house be willing to allow it."

Mary stood looking at the man as he leaned heavily on the chair near him, regaining his feet. When
he stood fully, he was nearly a head taller than she

was. "My late husband was at that same battle," she said.

"I offer my sincerest condolences. I lost my father at the battle and was taken as a prisoner of war. I left Illinois and have been following General Thomas for many weeks now."

"Why?" Curiosity glinted in her eyes. She cast them down to the floor.

"I had hoped to exact revenge on General Thomas for my father's death."

Mary looked up and met his gaze. "Why would you tell me this? I am a union supporter and could have Thomas' army here in no time."

Matthias took a step toward her and looked at her with unwavering eyes. "Even should you have manner to call them, I would be gone before the first soldier set foot out of camp."

She met his gaze, a wisp of something whirling between them. "Sir, I will offer you a hot meal, but then you must leave. This township is not a place where your cause is looked kindly upon. It is not safe for you here." She crossed into the kitchen.

"Your kindness is much appreciated," Matthias said from behind me as I turned to watch her. He came into the kitchen and sat down in one of the chairs.

I blinked and the scene changed. The man was sitting in the same chair, yet he was now wearing a clean white shirt and his hair was combed back. His beard was gone and his blue eyes were absolutely dazzling. Matthias leaned across the table to Mary, who was now wearing a yellow dress, her long hair spilling down her back in shiny blue-black waves. She smiled as he took her hand, her eyes full of love for the man sitting in the chair. She opened her mouth to speak.

"St. Louis!" she said, looking up at me. I gasped and felt myself falling. I closed my eyes, and when I opened them, I was lying on the floor of the kitchen, looking up at Evie's worried face. "St. Louis!" she shouted again. The kitchen was back to normal, except I noticed as I sat up that it looked much darker in the house.

"Holy crap!" Evie shouted. "You've been lying there for half an hour! Are you okay?"

"I was watching what happened," I said, rubbing my eyes.

"What do you mean what happened?" Evie yanked me to my feet.

"I mean, I saw Mary and I saw Matthias, and I saw how they met." I looked at Evie. "And I saw how they were falling in love."

Evie peered at me for a full minute. "Okay, St. Louis, I get it, but it's getting seriously late and your dad is going to start worrying. Can you walk?" she asked, offering her arm.

"I'm fine," I said, testing my legs gingerly. "Let's go."

I followed Evie around the edge of the parlor again, looking at the fireplace that had once been filled with the warm yellow glow of a fire and at the front door through which Mary had met her love. I walked through the woods as if I was in a trance. Before I knew it, we were standing at my car. It was nearly midnight.

I felt so full of sadness. It was only after we had driven back into the lights of town that I began to feel better. Evie had been uncharacteristically quiet on the drive to town.

"Are you okay?" I asked, glancing at her.

She was staring out of the window. "I'm fine," she said. "I think the better question, though, is are *you* okay? I mean, I'm used to your weird stuff, St. Louis, but that was really, really weird. It was like I couldn't wake you up."

"Are you sure I was out for that long?" I asked. "I mean, it felt like only a few minutes."

"Yeah."

"Well, now we know where her house is."

"Tristan and Andy are going to freak out when we tell them."

I nodded.

"You okay with going back out there?"

I nodded again. I didn't tell Evie that, now that I had seen Mary, there was nothing that could keep me from going back and finding out the rest of her story.

CHAPTER 18

The day before Christmas, Dad and I spent hours cooking and cleaning. The sun shone down all day, filling the house with brightness and a hopeful feeling. The snow melted outside, the dark muddy earth in the yard showing through in all the places not shaded by the house or trees. Andy and Tristan showed up around three, bearing gifts and smiles. Evie showed them in and put their presents under the enormous tree my dad insisted would fit in the living room. Several trims later, it had finally fit, although it did lean to the left a little and there had been no room for a star on top.

The doorbell rang just as we were sitting down to eat. Dad tossed his napkin on the table next to his plate and raised an eyebrow. "Nobody touches anything until I get back." He looked meaningfully at Andy who guiltily placed a roll back into the basket. Dad went to answer the door and I heard his voice as it got louder and louder.

We all looked at each other and headed to the living room.

Standing on the front porch was Evie's mom, obviously drunk, sporting the shortest skirt I had ever seen in real life.

"I came to see my daughter and I'm going to see her," Evie's mom said to my dad, pointing a long red fingernail into the middle of his chest. "And if you don't let me see her," she gestured wildly at the car and almost lost her balance, "Bob will come up here and make sure I get to see her."

My dad filled up the doorway with his six foot two frame, almost daring her to come in. He spoke very softly, but there was an undercurrent of danger in his voice. "I am very sorry, Ms. Patton, but you are currently in violation of a personal protection order I filed on behalf of Genevieve. I will be forced to call the police if you do not vacate the premises immediately."

Evie stood next to me and I could feel a sort of electricity coming off her. She drew herself up straight and marched over to the front door. "Excuse me, Mr. A," she said, "I need to talk to my mother."

My dad looked down at her with concern in his eyes. "I can call the police."

"It's okay, really."

He stepped aside and Evie walked out onto the porch.

"Baby girl!" Evie's mom held her arms wide, "come on home with me, okay? Bob's going to be staying with us for a while and he's real nice. You'll like him, I promise. Come on, baby. It's Christmas Eve." I watched as Evie's mom gathered her in a hug. Evie stayed stiff and wouldn't make eye contact with her mother. Finally, her mom stepped away, steadying herself on the porch railing.

"Mom," Evie said, her voice calm, "I have asked all my life for one thing on Christmas. I have wanted to have a parent that takes care of me, doesn't hit me, and doesn't let her boyfriends touch me." She took a step toward her mother, her voice rising a notch. "And, you have never given me that gift in sixteen years. This Christmas, I have that. I have a family that cares about me and loves me. They're going to help me find Daddy and then I'm leaving you, and I'm not ever coming back!"

"Oh, yeah? They love you, huh? They're going to help you find your daddy?"

"Ms. Patton, that's enough," my dad said. "It is time for you to go now."

She smiled a hateful smile and turned to Evie. "He left you, too. Don't you forget that!" she spat, curling her lip back from her yellow teeth. "Your Daddy don't want you!"

Evie looked like she had been punched. She looked up at my dad. Her eyes were rimmed with tears. "Is that true?"

"No, Genevieve, I don't think so, but we haven't been able to contact him yet. We're still looking because," he rubbed the back of his neck and looked at me, "I didn't want to tell either of you until things were more certain, but I started paperwork the last time I was in St. Louis to adopt Genevieve."

I felt tears burn my eyes and a smile turned the corners of my mouth. A lump grew in my throat and I nodded.

Dad turned his attention back to Evie. "We want you to stay with us, dear."

Evie threw her arms around my dad's shoulders and hugged him.

Dad looked up over Evie's head. "I want you to turn around and go home, Ms. Patton. We love Genevieve and we want her to be part of our family. Merry Christmas."

He and Evie turned their back on her mom and walked back into the house. Dad closed the door. We heard a car door slam and tires skidding in the melting snow as the car raced out of the driveway.

Evie turned to us and drew her lips into a forced smile. "So, my mom..." Her voice faded and she looked at me helplessly.

I shook my head. "You don't have to do that, Evie. You don't have to make excuses for her ever again."

Tristan cast a meaningful look at Andy and they headed back into the kitchen.

Dad looked down at her. "Genevieve, I meant what I said. We want you here."

Tears glistened in her eyes. "I want to be here. And, face it, you guys would starve without my mad cooking skills."

"Let's eat?" I asked.

"Yeah, let's eat."

After we had eaten until we were stuffed, the dishes had been cleaned, and the refrigerator filled with leftovers, we all headed upstairs to digest. Andy and Tristan were watching *It's a Wonderful Life* and Evie sat on the futon, legs drawn up to her chest.

"When should we head out?" Andy asked.

"I don't know. Evie?" I looked over at my friend from my perch on the bed. "Evie?"

"Huh?"

"Do you still feel like going tonight?" I asked. "It might help get your mind off...things."

"Yeah, we should go before it gets dark," she said absently, turning to look out the window again.

"Marissa!" Dad called from downstairs. "Someone's here to see you."

"Coming!" I shouted down the stairs.

"Will you be ready to leave after this?" Evie asked.

"Uh, yeah. Yeah, we can go in a few minutes."

Downstairs, standing in the kitchen was Grant wearing a Santa hat and looking utterly and ridiculously handsome. I ran and threw my arms around his neck.

"Merry Christmas." He gathered me into a hug.

"You want anything to eat? We have a ton of leftovers." We sat down at the table and I squinted at him. "I thought you had to work at the flower shop tonight?"

"I am," he winked. "I asked Justin if I could sneak out to say hi to my girl on Christmas Eve. Besides," he rolled his eyes, "we already delivered all the flowers for midnight mass." He looked down. "This looks nice," he said, reaching across the table to rub the sun and moon pendant between his rough fingers and thumb. His hand slid down to the tabletop and he left it there, palm up. I put my hand inside and smiled with the warmth I felt as he closed his fingers around mine.

"Ew, gross!" my dad yelled up the stairs as he came in the kitchen to refill his coffee cup. "Guys, they're holding hands down here!" He winked at me as he walked back to the living room.

"I should get going," Grant said, standing up. "I really wanted to see you for a minute."

"I have something for you. Wait here." I retrieved his gift from under the tree and shoved it in his hands. "Here. I've never really bought anything for a boy for Christmas. I mean, for my cousins and stuff, but not for, like, a..."

"A boyfriend?"

"Yeah, that."

He ripped into the paper and pulled out the scarf and gloves. "These are great! I lost my last pair of gloves while I was helping put up hay for the winter." He put them on and clapped them together with a fuzzy pop.

I leaned over and wrapped the scarf around his neck, using it to pull him forward for a kiss.

"Mmmm," he said, pushing in his chair. "Yeah, I really have to go now." He smiled, tossing his hair out of his eyes. "Another kiss like that and Justin will have to close by himself tonight." He headed out the back door, stopping for one more kiss before getting into his car and driving away.

"Merry Christmas," I whispered after him.

A few minutes later, we were all standing in the kitchen.

My dad regarded us for a moment. "You guys look like you're up to positively no good."

"Remember, Dad, I told you, they're having a skating party tonight at the roller rink in Eagleton?" I said, feeling my face flush red with the lie.

"Well, be careful. You know, seventy-six percent of skating accidents happen when people skate backwards," he said, a smile in his voice.

"And now, I'm leaving, because you're making fun of me."

"I'll see you a little later. Don't be out too late. Santa won't leave presents if you aren't asleep when he gets here."

"Bye, Dad, love you."

In Andy's truck, it was quiet. I looked around and narrowed my eyes. "So, I can't help but notice that no one's talking. I guess that means Evie told you what happened yesterday at the house?"

"She did," Tristan said. "Are you sure you feel like going back out there tonight?"

"I'll be fine."

"We need to make sure someone is with you at all times, so if it happens again..." Andy's voice trailed off.

"Yeah," Tristan chirped in again, "I'll make sure I'm with her all night. I won't leave your side, Marissa."

"Thanks," I said.

We followed the dark road out to the cemetery again. The huge tires on Andy's truck had trouble holding onto the gravel a few times and he concentrated, his eyes never leaving the soupy surface. He pulled off as far as he could to park and got out to survey his tires. "We should be able to get out of here. I threw a bale of straw in the back in case we have trouble."

"I have Triple A," I offered.

Andy looked at me and then dropped his head and shook it. "Here," he said, handing Tristan a bag from the toolbox.

I sat on the tailgate and pulled my boots on over my jeans.

Evie sat next to me doing the same. She pulled her hair up in a ponytail and smiled at me. "Ready?"

I nodded. The moon, low in the sky, dipped from behind a cloud and I wondered for a moment if the crying would happen again tonight. I decided that it was a small price to pay to help Mary. My heart hurt for her. She didn't deserve to be trapped in such pain. I buttoned my jacket and hopped down, my feet squishing into the mud. We pulled our back-packs out of the bed of the truck and put them on.

Evie and I led the way along the road to the for-est. Dusk gathered around us, the warmth of the af-ternoon losing its hold. It still wasn't nearly as cold as the night before and I yanked the hat I had been wearing off as I started sweating.

We heard the creek before we got to it. The rush of water created a backdrop as we walked along through the shadowy woods. As we got nearer to the bridge, the clouds released their grasp on the moon again and it shone down, lighting the bridge with an unearthly glow. The wailing began, quieter this time, but somehow more insistent. I thought I picked up a word, a name, and I gulped. It sounded like my own. I opened my mouth to tell Evie this, but snapped it shut and shook my head. *That's crazy.* I swallowed and watched as Tristan and Andy picked their way down to the creek.

The water tumbled through the valley, angry and brown, white foam rising in peaks along the edges. It flowed fast and steady, sticks jutting up from its surface as they were swept downstream. We stood looking at the bridge. It moved and shifted as the water flowed underneath. The bridge only cleared the water by about a foot and the sound of debris scratching along its bottom was unnerving. I shuddered.

Tristan turned to look back at me. "Are you okay?" he shouted above the sound.

I nodded and bit my bottom lip.

He turned and picked his way across the bridge. Andy and I were behind him. Evie was last, and when her feet were on solid ground on the other side, I let out the breath I had been holding. The crying stopped, but the temperature dropped significantly and the wind lilted around me, caressing my face with icy fingers. The moon disappeared and we all pulled out flashlights, their beams cutting through the gathering darkness. We walked up the hill, away from the creek.

"Wicked!" Andy said as we emerged into the clearing and he caught his first glimpse of the house. "This is so cool!" He made his way up onto the porch and pulled out his camera. "Lead the way, ghost lady." He smiled, nodding at me.

I took a deep breath and Tristan took my arm. We headed into the parlor together. It was infinitely creepier and felt darker than it had the evening before. More ominous. *Like something's lying in wait.* I shuddered as I led the way into the kitchen.

Andy and Evie started looking around, Andy providing a running commentary into the camera as he filmed. "A true antebellum house, this is where Mary lived and fell in love with a Confederate soldier named Matthias some one hundred fifty years ago..."

Tristan and I watched from the doorway to the kitchen.

Marissa.

"What?" I turned to Tristan.

"What? What?" he answered.

"You said my name."

"No, I didn't."

"Well, someone did," I said, loud enough for Evie and Andy to hear.

"We didn't say your name, St. Louis. Where did it come from?"

I pointed up, gooseflesh breaking out on my arms.

Andy pointed his flashlight up the stairs. Dust particles floated in the light.

"We have to go up there now, don't we?" I asked. I instantly regretted saying anything about hearing my name. The pressure from upstairs pushed down on me with a heaviness that was palpable.

Andy nodded.

We walked up the stairs, the coldness building with each step. My ears popped and Tristan gripped my hand tightly, his body close to mine. Andy led the way, stepping gingerly on each riser before putting all of his weight on it. About six steps up, an entire stair was missing and we all held our breath as he stepped over it onto the next riser.

After a precarious climb, we stood in a hallway, or in what was left of one anyway. The entire back wall of the house had fallen into the backyard, a pile of bricks and shards of glass lying below. A tree grew up through the open space, spreading skeletal branches through the slats on the back of a chair, tilting it at an odd angle. The hallway dipped dangerously to the left. Andy took a step and the floor groaned in protest. He leapt back to the stairs and waited there uncertainly.

"Let me," I said, sliding my backpack off. "I weigh the least and maybe I can make it over there." I gestured to the room at the end of the hallway. A door hanging from the corner by one set of hinges hid its interior.

"I don't think that's a good idea," Tristan said, not letting go of my arm.

"I don't think so, either, St. Louis. What if what happened earlier happens again when you're in there? We won't be able to get to you."

"I'll be fine," I said. I wasn't sure if it was the adrenaline or the strength of my friends that I was drawing upon, but suddenly I wasn't afraid.

For once in my life, I wasn't afraid.

Marissssa. The voice came again. This time, I was sure it was coming from behind the door.

"I'll be fine," I said again, prying Tristan's hand from my arm. "Let me take that." I nodded toward Andy's camera. Somewhat reluctantly, he handed it over to me. I started across the hallway, stopping periodically while the house settled under me. I made it successfully to the door and turned to give the crew a thumbs up. I yanked at the door, but it wouldn't budge. Setting the camera down at my feet, I used both hands to jimmy the door out far enough that I could get inside. I picked up the camera, and with one last look at my friends, I headed into the room.

CHAPTER 19

In the room, I saw Mary. She sat in a chair by the window, knitting. Her hair was drawn up and she was wearing the most beautiful ivory dress. The bodice had pearl buttons up the front and the skirt swirled out around her legs, moving as she rocked gently. Mary looked onto the branches of a flowering tree and I could almost smell the warm spring breeze as it fluttered through the lace curtains and across the simple bedroom. In a chair near the other window, Matthias sat, reading a book and looking up occasionally to smile at Mary. He was dressed in a pair of tan pants and a blue cotton shirt, his features soft and almost glowing.

I gasped, almost forgetting to film. I spun the camera up and watched through the viewer. The camera showed only a dark decrepit room. I looked up again.

"I love you," she said to Matthias.

He leaned over and touched her face in a gesture so gentle and loving that tears welled up in my eyes.

Suddenly, something seemed to catch Mary's eye outside the window. She stood up, knocking over her yarn basket, a look of horror on her face. She whirled around to face Matthias, a wild terror taking over her features.

"Hide!" she hissed.

Matthias crawled under the bed, pulling the coverlet down around the side. I could hear his scared breathing coming from underneath. Mary placed her knitting in the basket and made sure Matthias was tucked away before hurrying out of the room. The pounding that came from the front door was insistent. Matthias began to pray under the bed. My stomach churned. There were muffled voices downstairs and then the sound of boots stomping on the stairs. Matthias grew deathly quiet.

Suddenly, the door was thrown open behind me and a man stepped in, scanning the room. He wore a blue uniform lined with brass buttons in two rows down the front, stars adorning the patches on his shoulders. His hair was graying, as was his thick mustache. The heels of his boots clicked on the floorboards.

Mary appeared in the doorway. "Perhaps, I can offer Mr. Thomas an iced tea -"

"*General* Thomas," he corrected, striding around the room. He walked over to the chairs where Mary and Matthias had been sitting moments before and looked at Mary. "It was reported that a known Confederate soldier was seen on your premises not two days before by the good Mister Renthroe. He claims he saw this wanted man tending to your fence." The general looked down at her, a sneer curling his lip. "Now, Mrs. Douglas, surely you know the penalty for harboring an enemy of the United States, don't you?"

Mary nodded demurely.

"And, I wouldn't have to tell you what shame that would bring upon your dead husband's name, rest his soul?"

Again, Mary nodded.

General Thomas made his way over to the bed, his eyes watching Mary's face the whole time. The toe of his boot brushed the coverlet.

"But if," his voice softened, "a poor widow woman like yourself was being held captive by a Confederate heathen, we could arrange for her to suffer no consequences at all."

Mary stood stone-faced.

Suddenly, there was movement from below the bed. Matthias crawled out and stood solemnly in front of the Union officer. A small strangled cry escaped from Mary.

"Sir," Matthias said, "I am, indeed, a deserter of the Army of the Confederacy and as such, I ask that you seek mercy rather than vengeance. This dear woman had no choice but to take me in as I threatened her life."

"Matthias, no!" Mary shouted, taking a step toward him.

Matthias shot her a warning glance, his blue eyes sparking.

The General looked from Matthias to Mary and back again. He narrowed his eyes. "I see. Thusly, since you are no longer wearing the uniform of a soldier, you will not be afforded the rights of one. Be you labeled as an enemy of the state, a spy. Do you know the punishment for this transgression?"

Matthias nodded. He turned to Mary. "It is but a term in a labor camp. I will be released before the first snow begins to fall." The muscle in his jaw worked as he sent a tendril of love to her, the wisp moving through the space between them and winding its way around her. Her chin trembled and she blinked several times.

"Take him away." General Thomas motioned to the soldiers standing at the door. Matthias walked past Mary and into the waiting hands of the soldiers. They grabbed him and shoved him down the stairs.

Tears streamed down Mary's face. She stood still, not making eye contact with the General.

"Be thou thankful for our service to your family today, dear woman," the general snarled. "It would be a shame to have left a woman of your standing at the mercy of such an animal."

He left the room and his boots pounded down the stairs. Mary stood staring at the door, her eyes locking with mine for a moment before she dropped her head. I shivered. An undercurrent of something sinister floated around the periphery. The door slammed downstairs and Mary looked up, tears streaming down her face. She crept to the window and looked out. Hoof beats faded as Mary watched out the window.

A moment later, she turned and ran from the room. I could hear her running down the stairs, and then she too ran out the front door into the waiting woods. I dashed to the window and looked down.

The soldiers led Matthias on the road, away from the house. Mary hid near the front porch and then took off, cutting through the woods around them, her long white skirt flowing behind her.

I lost sight of her as she bounded through the trees and I whirled around, plunged back into the darkness of real time. It took a second for my eyes to adjust and for me to get my bearings, but then I squeezed through the door and ran across the hallway, disregarding the floor as part of it caved in and went tumbling down with a crash.

"We have to follow her!" I yelled as I pushed past Evie and Tristan. I thrust the camera into Andy's hands and took the stairs two at a time, their flashlight beams waving wildly on the walls behind me as I ran. The group ran after me as I headed out the door and through the woods. I stopped for a moment, looking around for any glimpse of Mary. Then, to my right, I saw a fold of her dress as she ran down a hill. I followed and soon could see her clearly, as she ran. As we crested the hill, I could see the road below. The soldiers led Matthias toward the bridge, his hands tied by coarse rope behind his back.

Mary reached the hill above the bridge, crouching behind a tree, hidden from sight.

I crouched next to her, the sound of her panting loud in my ears. I stared at her face. She stared down at the soldiers and her dear Matthias.

He lied to you, didn't he?

Mary turned to me and regarded me with gentle eyes. They were filled with the sadness of decades of regret. She nodded, then turned back to watch the scene unfold.

"She's seeing something," I heard Evie whisper to Tristan and Andy as they came up behind me.

I felt her hand on my shoulder. I reached up to hold onto it and I looked at my best friend with tear-filled eyes. "It's happening all over again," I whispered, "and I don't know how to stop it. I don't know how to help her."

"It's okay, St. Louis. We can leave now. We can go," she said with urgency.

"No," I said. "I *have* to help her."

I could hear Mary crying next to me and I tried to reach out a hand to touch her, but I only felt open space. I followed her gaze as she looked down on the road below.

Matthias was walking along and he turned to look back at the house. It was no longer in view and he turned to the general. His voice was strong. "Thank you for heeding my words and waiting until my dearest Mary cannot see this travesty."

I watched with horror as the general got off his horse and walked over to Matthias, grabbing the end of the rope that circled his wrists. He led Matthias over to the bridge, followed by his soldiers.

Mary trembled as she watched the general tie a noose into one end of the rope, and then he tossed it over a strong limb of the tree that leaned out over the bridge. He drew the noose up tightly around Matthias' neck.

I watched alongside Mary as her lover was shoved off the side of the bridge. His body fell straight down and there was a sickening sound as the rope snapped taut. Matthias' body writhed once and then hung limply, swinging slightly below the bridge. Mary fell to the ground next to me, sobbing silently. My heart ached and tears rolled down my face. I watched as the soldiers mounted their horses and crossed the bridge. Some spat at Matthias' body and some took off their hats as they passed. The general didn't even look as he rode across. When they went over the hill, Mary stood and ran, crying and falling down the hill toward the bridge.

I followed, feeling like I was going to throw up at any moment. My heart hurt and I felt more tired than I had ever felt before. As I stumbled down the hill, the night closed in on the scene in front of me. I couldn't see or hear anything outside of this little circle of light in the middle of the bridge. In it, Mary was trying to pull Matthias up. She was crying so hard that she couldn't get a good grip on the rope. I watched as she tried again and again to lift him up. I could feel her desperation and her panic as she pulled and pulled, the rope tearing into the soft skin of her palms. I could see the blood as it streaked the rope. I reached out and put a hand on her shoulder.

"Mary," I whispered. She stopped and turned to look at me, her hair wild around her face. *Mary, he's gone now. It's okay. You can let him go. I know it's hard, Mary, but you have to let him go.* I could feel my heart break. I had let my mother go and I knew that it was harder than anything I had ever done. I watched as Mary looked down at the rope and then at her mangled hands. She let the rope go and stood on the bridge, peering down to her dear Matthias swinging below.

She turned to look at me, her eyes shifting. Something dark overtook them, and they deepened, turning the color of black ink, filling her eye sockets. Her lips drew back in a sneer and I saw rows of pointed teeth hiding beyond. She opened her mouth wide, the sound of a thousand screams emanating from her. I took a step away, my back hitting the side of the bridge. The sound of the rushing water below registered in my consciousness as Mary moved toward me.

Marissa. You're mine now.

"No!" I screamed, throwing my hands up in front of me.

Mary reached out, her essence pure evil.

I felt her hands pressing into my chest, pushing me back over the edge of the bridge. Behind me, I felt another set of hands, these warm and comforting, holding me steady. A flash of someone came into my line of sight and then Evie was in front of me, sheltering me from Mary's grasp. Evie splayed her hands, shoving Mary away. As she did, Evie lost her footing and fell backwards, her body breaking the rotten wood of the railing on the bridge. The wood made an awful splintering sound and I turned to see Evie falling into the water below. She grabbed onto the edge of the wood as the frigid water pulled her under. Her head came up for a moment and then the water drove her face first into the side of the bridge with a terrible cracking sound. Her eyes rolled back and her grip loosened.

I screamed and threw myself down on the bridge, grabbing her hand. The water yanked at my unconscious friend. I screamed for Andy and Tristan and heard them running down the hill. Her cold wet hand slipped in mine and I knew they would never make it in time.

There was an enormous ripping sound behind me and I turned to see Mary's figure fall to the ground. Something dark and sinister flew out of her and paused for a moment at the end of the bridge. It turned to look at me with an evil that turned my blood to ice. It stared at me through blood red eyes and then disappeared into the woods with a screeching sound that tore at my eardrums.

Then, Mary was beside me, her hands reaching out to help pull my best friend from the water. *Don't let go.*

I won't.

We pulled, Evie finally edging up onto the bridge, first her chest and middle, and then her legs. Andy and Tristan raced over and helped me pull Evie the rest of the way out of the water.

"Oh, no, Evie!" I screamed. Her face was a bloody mess and her nose looked broken. There was a huge gash on her forehead where she'd hit the bridge and her body was cold and lifeless. I sat back on my heels, tears streaming down my face.

Andy checked her breathing. "She's alive," he said, wrapping her in his coat. He lifted her from the bridge and cradled her in his arms. "Tristan, get Marissa." He began walking, Evie in his arms.

Tristan leaned down and looked into my eyes. "Marissa, honey, we have to get Evie to help, okay?"

I nodded numbly. The iciness of the water burned my hands and Tristan took them in his own, helping me stand on unsteady legs.

Thank you.

I turned to see Mary standing beside Matthias. They were smiling and holding one another. They turned and walked together back toward the house, fading into the mist.

I leaned on Tristan as he led me out of the woods and back to the truck. My eyes were heavy and my breaths hitched in my chest as I sobbed. Andy placed Evie in the truck. I climbed in and put her head on my lap, smoothing the wet hair from her face as Andy and Tristan climbed in and slammed the doors. Her lips were a nasty shade of blue and I held a handkerchief over the cut on her forehead. It turned dark with her blood. Andy gunned the engine and Tristan dialed the phone. He spoke with the 9-1-1 operator while Andy sped down the roads, his face grim.

We arrived at the emergency room and they wheeled Evie away. We answered all of the questions about what happened and my dad arrived, his face ashen with worry. He grabbed me and wrapped me in a hug.

I sobbed against his chest. "I-I'm so sorry. We were just trying to help!"

"We will talk later about what happened. Right now, I'm going to find out how Genevieve is."

Andy and Tristan perched on the edges of two chairs in the waiting room while my dad walked up to the counter. I stood in the middle of the floor, my stomach churning, lightheaded and feeling faint.

Dad paced for hours while we waited to hear about Evie. Finally, the doctor came out to talk to us. The words made no sense: "...medically induced coma to stop the brain from swelling..."

CHAPTER 20

I sat crossed legged on the carpet in my room. I held Evie's present in my hands. "I was going to give this to you on Christmas morning, but you know."

"Yeah, I know." We sat in silence for a minute. "So, open it now."

I smiled and slid my finger under the tape. "This feels weird."

"Well, I can't exactly do it myself, St. Louis."

I nodded and ripped off the paper. It fell to the floor and I opened the box, leaning over to show her.

She breathed in. "I love it. Seriously, it's perfect."

"Well, you need to get better soon so you can wear it." I nodded and placed it on the floor next to me. I took a deep breath. "Evie, why do you think Mary tried to hurt me?"

Evie was silent for a long time. "I don't think it was her."

"What was it?"

"I can't see ghosts but *I* was able to see whatever that thing was." She shuddered. "It was pure evil."

"You shouldn't have done what you did."

She laughed. "And let it kill my sister?"

"I'm not your sister yet."

"Might as well be."

I was quiet for a moment. "I saw it, too."

"I don't think it's gone."

I sighed. "I don't either." I stood up, rolling my head on my shoulders. Then, I leaned down to pick up the box with her necklace from the floor.

"What did you see? When you went into the room alone?"

I closed my eyes and swallowed. "I saw the last moments of Matthias and Mary's life," I whispered.

"You helped them, though, right?"

I nodded.

"And, you're going to help others, right?"

I nodded again. "I don't think I have a choice in this now, Evie."

"*We* don't have a choice, you mean. It all changes now, though. Ghost Hunters Society is going to help people, not just investigate hauntings."

"I guess," I said. Then I paused, tilting my head. "You already know where we're going next, don't you?"

She shook her head. "Not where, yet. I'm still getting used to this stuff. But I know there's a little girl that needs our help."

There was a knock on the door downstairs, followed shortly by a soft knock at my door.

"Come in," I said.

Dad poked his head in. "Hey, Peanut. Andy and Tristan are here. We're heading over to the hospital to see Evie in about five minutes."

"She isn't there," I mumbled.

Evie snickered beside me. "Understatement of the year, St. Louis."

Dad crossed the room and put his arm around my shoulders. "I know it seems like it's not her, but I know she's in there and she'll hear you if you talk to her. Okay?"

I nodded. "Yeah, I'll go. I'll be ready in a few minutes."

"She's going to be all right," he said, heading out the door.

I swallowed. "I know, Dad. I know."

ADRIA WATERS

Watch for the next Ghost Hunters Society book:
The Devil Doll
December 2016

Acknowledgements

My unending love, admiration, and appreciation go to my husband and my son. I would never have the strength to do this without you. You are my rocks.

Thank you to my writing buddies, Amanda Booloodian and Christina Benedict, who have seen this book grow from idea to printed page. Thank you also to the Columbia Novelist Group, especially CJ Weiland, Brianna Boes, and Liz Schulte, whose critiques and thoughts were so very helpful through the writing of this book. Much appreciation to my amazing beta readers, Roger Bolle, Julie Bolle, Elizabeth Zumwalt, Trey Coloney, and Brenda Coffman, who gave their time, feedback, and encouragement.

Thank you again to my wonderful editor, Frankie Rhodes, for her patience, caring insights, and wonderful attention to detail. Thanks, as well, to Covered Creatively for another amazing cover design and to Vicki Deiter for her formatting expertise.

ABOUT THE AUTHOR

Adria Waters is a paranormal enthusiast who has been seeing ghosts all her life. Her greatest moment was doing an overnight investigation at an abandoned prison with the cast of Ghost Hunters from SyFy. When she's not hunting ghosts, she loves torturing her family with road trips across the country to see everything from Mount Rushmore to Disneyworld and every sightseeing opportunity in between. A huge Harry Potter fan, she spent days in Universal Studios wandering the streets of Hogsmeade with Butterbeer in hand, muttering spells under her breath and believing, if only for a moment, that the wand she held might actually turn someone into a frog. Adria lives in Missouri with her very patient husband, her not so patient son, two cats who insist that they are human, and various little spirits that pop up to say "hello" once in a while.

You can find out more about Adria and her writing, including upcoming releases, on www.AdriaWaters.com
You can also find her on Facebook: AdriaWatersWrites,
Twitter: @AdriaWaters1, and
Amazon: Adria Waters